Applause for Nova Rocks!

"Told with a lot of humor and teen angst."

—*School Library Journal*

"A fresh, hip, and charming tale that is laugh-out-loud funny."

—Elizabeth Cody Kimmel, author of
Lily B. on the Brink of Cool

"Readers will . . . cheer Nova on as she seeks the courage to be herself."

—*St. Louis Post-Dispatch*

"Star Sisterz will help the next generation of girls by offering them stories of courage, kindness, imagination, and hope."

—Mary Pipher, author of *Reviving Ophelia:
Saving the Selves of Adolescent Girls*

Kudos to Carmen Dives In

"Parents will approve, and girls likely will love them."

—*Salem Statesman Journal*

"Exactly what a series read should be—fun and fast-paced . . ."

—Kidsreads.com

"Once you read one, you'll want to read them all!"

—Bookloons.com

Bravo for Bright Lights for Bella

"Once again, Star Sisterz sets just the right tone for a series book."

—Kidsreads.com

"Fresh, fun, and unique. Lana Perez has an uncanny ability to capture in her writing the way a young teenager thinks."

—Bookloons.com

Raves for Rani and the Fashion Divas

"A well-written, enjoyable story about figuring out who you really are and what price you're willing to pay for popularity."

—Kidsreads.com

Debra Green

MIRRORSTONE

MAYA MADE OVER
©2007 Wizards of the Coast, Inc.

All characters in this book are fictitious. Any resemblance to actual persons, living or dead, is purely coincidental.

This book is protected under the copyright laws of the United States of America. Any reproduction or unauthorized use of the material or artwork contained herein is prohibited without the express written permission of Wizards of the Coast, Inc.

Published by Wizards of the Coast, Inc. STAR SISTERZ, MIRRORSTONE, and their respective logos are trademarks of Wizards of the Coast, Inc., in the U.S.A. and other countries.

Printed in the U.S.A.

The sale of this book without its cover has not been authorized by the publisher. If you purchased this book without a cover, you should be aware that neither the author nor the publisher has received payment for this "stripped book."

Cover art by Taia Morley
Interior art by A. Friend
First Printing: April 2007
Library of Congress Catalog Card Number: 2005935551

9 8 7 6 5 4 3 2 1

ISBN: 978-0-7869-4162-9
620-95741740-001-EN

U.S., CANADA,
ASIA, PACIFIC, & LATIN AMERICA
Wizards of the Coast, Inc.
P.O. Box 707
Renton, WA 98057-0707
+1-800-324-6496

EUROPEAN HEADQUARTERS
Hasbro UK Ltd
Caswell Way
Newport, Gwent NP9 0YH
GREAT BRITAIN
Please keep this address for your records

Visit our website at **www.mirrorstonebooks.com**

For my daughter Sarah,
a karate-loving, trivia-spouting tomboy
who I love just the way she is.

Chapter 1

Mr. Beebe was sleeping again. He leaned back at his desk with a newspaper covering his face. He snored like an out-of-control high-speed train. The newspaper shook up and down with each loud snort he made.

Sigh. Mr. Beebe obviously didn't care about Brain Bowl. Was I the only person at our school who did? Even my own teammates didn't seem concerned. If they cared about Brain Bowl as much as I did, they would have been here in Mr. Beebe's classroom by now, suffering with me through our worthless faculty advisor's sluggish grunts and groans.

Where the heck were my teammates anyway? I dragged a chair to the open doorway and sat down. I scanned the kids walking through the hallway, looking for two slightly chubby freshmen with bright blue eyes, dirty blond hair, and glasses. Dirk is a few inches taller than Daisy and his complexion is a little ruddier, but otherwise they look like twins. I also searched for a dark-eyed girl with maple skin and a serious expression: Rani Sen.

But mostly I had my eyes open for a long-legged, thick-haired, tall-as-a-tower guy with a swagger and an easy, musical laugh. That would be Bud Bloom. *Sigh again.* Just saying his name in my head made my heart beat almost as loud as Mr. Beebe's snores.

Where was Bud? I needed him—I mean, the team needed him.

Stop wasting time, Maya, I lectured myself. The Brain Bowl County Championship game is less than a month away. Get out your flashcards and study while you can.

I took off my backpack and felt myself relax a tiny bit. Not that I ever really relaxed, but taking the pack off helped. (After all, it weighed eighteen and a half pounds on average, according to my recent calculations.) I unzipped my pack, pulled out my flashcards, and started studying the Academy Awards. I got stuck on "Name the four movies for which Katherine Hepburn won an Oscar." I knew *The Lion in Winter, Guess Who's Coming* to *Dinner,* and *On Golden Pond,* but what was that fourth one? How could I concentrate with Mr. Beebe snorting like a deranged hog? And where the heck was everyone on my team? Think, Maya, think. Was the last movie *Little Women? The Philadelphia Story?* What if this were a tiebreaker question at the big game?

I turned over the flashcard. *Morning Glory.* I definitely needed to study more.

Ack!

Two gigantic hands covered my face, blinding me. A brutal attacker had come to our school and chosen me as his victim!

I shot out my arm behind me as hard and as fast as I could, elbowing the brute in the stomach. Then, while he was hunched over in back of me, I used my right hand to grab his right wrist, clamped my left hand on his right shoulder, stepped behind him, bent his elbow, and locked up the attacker in a classic hammerlock.

Yes! I had practiced this move in karate class for years, but was never forced to employ it in a life-or-death situation. I had this bad guy in a death grip. I couldn't wait to tell Sensei George what I'd done. I might not even have to tell him. My heroism would probably be all over the newspapers. Reading about my bravery could be Sensei George's proudest moment. And my little sister, Tiffany, would admire me even more than she did now.

I proudly looked down at my foe.

Oh no. Oh no, oh no, oh no. My alleged attacker, who had merely put his hands over my eyes, was Bud Bloom. This had to be the most mortifying moment of my entire fourteen years of existence—unless you counted the time when I was three and threw up all over my preschool teacher. But at that age, I didn't even know what mortification was. Plus, my preschool teacher wasn't the love of my life.

Bud Bloom was, though he didn't know it. He starred in my fantasies involving walking hand in hand on the beach or, alternatively, kissing passionately on the cover of *Teen People,* after being named International Brain Bowl Champions. He gave me goose bumps—not always, but approximately 85 percent of the time that he was reasonably close to me. Bud Bloom was finally in my arms, but not the way I'd dreamed it. It was more like a nightmare.

"What are you doing to Bud?" Rani asked. "I hope you didn't hurt him."

Great. To magnify my mortification, I had a witness.

Make that three witnesses. I heard the distinctive guffaws of Daisy and Dirk.

✹ ✿ ✹

I dropped my arms. My cheeks were so hot you probably could have fried an egg on them.

"I didn't realize that was you," I half-whispered to Bud.

Bud rubbed his stomach where I'd elbowed it. "I was just joking around with you," he said. "No need to attempt to kill me."

"I am so-o-o-o sorry," I said to my flashcards. I should have apologized to Bud's face, but there was just no way I could look him in the eyes. He must have known I was apologizing to him, not my flashcards (although he had accused me of being in love with them before).

Bud put his large hands on my burning cheeks and moved my head up so I had to look at him.

Had I hurt him? He didn't appear injured or even particularly upset. His face looked the same as it always did—gorgeous. One look into his dark, twinkly eyes and I could hardly breathe.

Bud, on the other hand, seemed to be breathing just fine. He even managed to let loose his easygoing laugh, as if I hadn't just held him in a semi–death grip. "I always thought you wanted to work us to death," he said. "I didn't know you'd resort to actual physical assault."

How could he be so calm? I certainly was not ready to laugh. I knew I wouldn't be able to laugh at that for a long time—quite possibly my entire life. I couldn't even force myself to smile. In fact, I was too embarrassed to do anything but stare at my flashcards.

I hoped this wouldn't get all over school. It was bad enough I was the only African-American Brain Bowl member with a brown belt in karate. If people found out I took down my six-foot-one male teammate, they'd think I was really bizarre. I bit my lip—an old habit I needed to break—and then explained that I thought some evildoer was trying to attack me.

"Bud, you do kind of look dangerous," Rani said. "You could be mistaken for an escaped convict on the run."

"This is how I always look," Bud said.

"Like you woke up three minutes before you had to leave for school," she said.

"Twelve minutes, actually, today," he said. "I even had time to shower."

"Obviously you did little else." Rani shook her head. "Your shirt is only half tucked in and your hair looks absolutely wild, like it hasn't seen a comb for months."

Daisy laughed. "And your pants are too short. They also give you the escaped convict look, like those are the same ones you bought before your jail sentence."

If someone talked like that about me, I'd have probably run from the room and burst into tears. But Bud just laughed again. He was so brave.

I wished the girls would be nicer to Bud. And it wasn't just because I liked the guy. Dissension and criticism could ruin a team faster than you could say, "Wrong answer." Getting clobbered by me, a brown belt, was enough trauma for one day.

Besides, I thought he looked just fine. Better than just fine, actually. I loved his wild, curly hair and his corduroy pants that revealed an inch and a half of his classy argyle socks. Of course, I'd never admit to anyone that I thought he was cute.

I checked his expression to see if the girls had upset him. (And also because I liked checking him out.) He didn't seem upset at all. In fact, I didn't think he'd even been paying attention to them, or to me.

"Right back at you," he called to someone through the open doorway. He sounded the opposite of upset, whatever that was. Overjoyed, I supposed.

No wonder. The person in the hallway was Lindsey Jacques. She was smiling at him with her bright white teeth and swinging her pink purse, which perfectly matched the pink suede boots that showed off her long, shapely legs.

No wonder Bud wasn't upset. I doubt any guy could get upset around Lindsey Jacques. She was everything I wasn't. If you looked up my name in the dictionary, it would say: Brainy, black, and blah. Antonym: Lindsey Jacques. I bet Lindsey would never go to school without makeup, or carry a fanny pack instead of a purse, or wear no-name sneakers.

Lindsey walked toward us. Toward Bud Bloom, I suspected. Her scent was noticeable from ten feet away and I had to admit she smelled good. She always wears this cinnamony perfume. Between her aroma and her looks, she is a total guy magnet. Boys couldn't have been more attracted if she wore a wide-screen TV on Superbowl Sunday. And it isn't just her nice perfume and extensive wardrobe that makes her a high school hottie. It is Lindsey Jacques's entire self—her soft giggles, her long, wavy blond hair that sparkles in the sunshine, and her fashionable clothes that fit her just right and never appear to get stained or wrinkled, or both, like mine do.

I glanced at my T-shirt. I'd spilled ketchup on it at lunchtime and tried to rub it off with water. But it had spread into a huge dark circle on the center of my shirt, like a bull's-eye for losers.

I hoped Lindsey wouldn't notice. She stood about

three and a half inches from Bud, batting her thick, dark eyelashes, pointing at Mr. Beebe, and giggling.

I was somewhat impressed that Lindsey could do three actions simultaneously: eyelash-batting, pointing, and giggling. I could barely walk and recite the Greek alphabet at the same time.

My teammates laughed at our faculty advisor and chatted, though they didn't attempt the additional action of eyelash-batting, like Lindsey did.

Ha-ha. Mr. Beebe snoring. Very funny. But not to me. Without a conscious adult in the room, I'd have to run the practice again. If Mrs. Bennett were here, she would have gotten my teammates to start preparing. I wished she'd come back from maternity leave already.

I checked my watch. It said 2:48 and twenty nine seconds. If we had begun practice at 2:35 and three seconds, when I first got here, we would have already had thirteen minutes and twenty-six seconds of knowledge under our belts.

"Guys, we need to get started," I announced.

Bud saluted me. "Aye, aye, drill sergeant."

Lindsey giggled. He gave her a dazzling smile in return.

Are Bud Bloom and Lindsey Jacques flirting with each other? I thought to myself. Great. Just great.

Bud probably imagined me in a military uniform, screaming at him to get to work. Drill sergeants were not the subjects of romantic interest, especially not for the very mellow Bud Bloom. Double especially, since he was talking to the opposite of drill sergeants, Lindsey Jacques. Triple especially, since she was wearing a white lace blouse and butterfly-patterned skirt, which even I realized made her look scrumptious and sweet. Argh!

As if to emphasize her scrumptious sweetness, Lindsey apologized for distracting us. Though she addressed her apology to all of us, I knew who was distracted the most: Bud.

It wasn't really Lindsey's fault. She couldn't help being pretty and perky and personable, not to mention scrumptiously sweet. It was probably hard having it all, including all the other girls' jealousy.

I wished I had her problems.

But I had more important problems, the most crucial of which was how to motivate my teammates. After all, I didn't join the Brain Bowl team to chitchat with people. I signed up so I could learn interesting facts, work with others toward a common goal, and hopefully beat the pants off every other team.

A moment after I waved good-bye to Lindsey, I announced, "Let's start with the Oscars. Who can name the movies for which Katherine Hepburn earned Academy Awards?"

Mr. Beebe let out a world-record loud snore.

"No, it's not *The Big Sleep*," Bud quipped.

Everyone laughed.

I joined in, hoping that Bud would notice that not only was I smart but I had a good sense of humor too.

Once the laughter died down, Dirk said, "*On Golden Pond,* that's easy. *Guess Who's Coming to Dinner*. And, uh. Hmm . . . That's about all I know."

I looked down at my flashcards. "Anyone else want to guess?"

"*The Lion in Winter* and *Morning Glory,*" Bud said.

Not only was Bud totally adorable, but under his cute, thick, curly hair he also had a colossal brain. What a guy.

"Maya. Is Bud right about the movies?" Rani asked me.

Oops. Talk about distracted. "Correct."

As usual, once I got everyone to start practicing, we did well. After about ten minutes studying the Academy Awards, we moved on to American presidents and then European royalty. The whole team was getting most of the questions right. I thought we might have a good shot at winning the County Championship.

After we studied countries in Africa, I suggested moving on to another place.

"How about some place cold? Where there's ice cream," Bud said.

"Good idea." I smiled at him. It was great to hear his enthusiasm for a change. "We haven't quizzed one another on Antarctica in a long time. But I can't think of any questions about ice cream."

Bud smiled back at me. "By suggesting someplace cold with ice cream, I meant that we could all walk over to Baskin-Robbins and celebrate a successful practice."

Everyone thought that was a great idea.

Everyone but me. I checked my watch. It was 3:56 and 28 seconds. We'd only been practicing an hour— actually, three minutes short of an hour. Maybe if my teammates hadn't been late, or if we hadn't wasted all that time in the beginning with small talk, Baskin-Robbins would be justified. But not as things were.

"How about this?" I suggested. "Thirty-seven minutes or so more practice, guys, and then we can talk about ice cream?" I thought I sounded very accommodating.

Not accommodating enough, apparently. Rani said that she was starving to death; Daisy said that her brain was holding a silent protest from all its effort; Dirk told me to lighten up, and Bud was whistling a tune, possibly, "Don't Worry, Be Happy." All the while, they were putting their study materials away in their backpacks.

"We can't quit now," I said.

Too late. All of my teammates were making their way out of the classroom.

Bud turned around and looked at me with his long-lashed midnight eyes. "Come on, Maya." he said. Actually, one might even classify that as begging.

If I wasn't so mad at him for cutting the practice short, I might have said yes. Instead, I shook my head. As they walked past me and out the door, I thought about how hard it was to be the only competitive person on the Brain Bowl team. And I thought about Baskin-Robbins, a place I had loved as a kid, and probably still would love if I ever had time to go there. I wondered if they still sold peppermint fudge ripple there. I also thought about Bud's long legs.

I got out an old test and turned to the science portion. I tried to study chemical compounds and reactions. But my mind was on my teammates, particularly the one who compounded my chemical reactions. After seven and a half fruitless minutes, I gathered up my Brain Bowl materials, stuffed them in my backpack, headed to the classroom door, and shoved it open.

"Practice over?" Mr. Beebe asked.

The second scare of the day. My whole body twitched. At least I didn't try to put the man in a hammerlock. Instead, I said, "I didn't realize you were awake. Unfortunately, yes, practice is over." I thanked him for the use of his classroom. He responded with a snore.

Could a person feel any more alone? I closed the door gently and shuffled through campus.

Chapter 2

As I was walking out, I saw Carmen Bernstein and Nova Darling sitting on the cement ledge under the high school marquee, chatting and smiling as if they hadn't a care in the world. Neither of them had an apathetic team to contend with or an upcoming County Championship competition.

I picked up my pace. If I got home by 4:20, I could play with my sister for forty minutes, and then get more practice in from 5:00 until dinnertime. I also had homework, of course, and I wanted to perfect my punches for karate class. Though judging my earlier victimization of Bud Bloom, I was pretty darn good already. Or bad, from Bud's point of view.

Carmen and Nova waved at me, and I returned the greeting.

"Hey, Maya, did you know you're famous?" Nova pointed to the marquee.

Huh? I looked up. The sign said: "Congratulations Bud, Daisy, Dirk, Maya, and Rani for making it to the County Championship Brain Bowl."

I tried to smile at Carmen and Nova, but I bet it came out looking grim. I was proud of myself and the team, of course, for making it so far. But I was also embarrassed. I knew other people thought that the Brain Bowl was geeky. And my name was associated with it in big letters for the entire school to read. If I had made it to the cheerleading finals or soccer playoffs, that would have been cool. But the Brain Bowl championship? The marquee might as well have said, "Maya Truitt is a nerd."

I wondered what my teammates thought of the sign. They must have noticed it on their way out, unless they were all too busy chatting and giggling and doing whatever else people do when they don't realize the County Championship game will be one of the biggest events of their lives.

I pictured my teammates with double scoops of ice cream at Baskin-Robbins. Knowing Bud, who ate like a garbage disposal, he probably ordered a triple scoop or a giant banana split.

I wished I'd gone with them. On the other hand, I also wished they'd wanted to study more. We would never win the championship by taking ice cream breaks. I tried to look on the bright side. At least losing would keep our names off the marquee.

I glanced at it one more time. *Whoa! What is that?* The message on the marquee had suddenly switched. It read:

Make up a slogan about yourself and promote yourself with it.

"Did you see that?" I asked Nova and Carmen.

"We're the ones who pointed it out to you," Nova said.

"I hope you do really well," Carmen said.

"Thanks, but I meant the slogan thing." I looked up at the marquee again. The message had changed back to the Brain Bowl one. I kept staring, but I didn't see the "Make up a slogan" message again. Weird.

Nova laughed. "You love seeing your name up there, don't you, Maya?"

Oh, geez. How long had I been staring? Embarrassment Central. "I . . . I . . . I have to go."

I headed for my house without looking back. Usually, during the walk home I try to recite facts we might be tested on during the Brain Bowl. But I just couldn't concentrate on studying, not after brutalizing Bud Bloom, being deserted for dessert, and seeing that strange sign at school. What was up with the marquee message?

Anyway, there was no way I was going to make up a slogan about myself. People would laugh at me, or sneer, or do a simultaneous laugh-sneer. I wondered what a simultaneous laugh-sneer would be like anyway. I looked around to make sure no one was nearby and tried one out.

Yes, a simultaneous laugh-sneer was possible. As an African-American brown belt Brain Bowl member, I was surprised I hadn't been subjected to one or two or a hundred yet. I might get some tomorrow, once everyone in school saw my name on the marquee.

If I was to make up a slogan about myself, what would it be?

After what happened at practice today, I wouldn't exactly call myself Queen of the Team. I was more suited for I Crush My Crush, World's Biggest Nerd, Call Me Drill Sergeant, or The Opposite of Lindsey Jacques. I sure wouldn't want the job of promoting myself after my afternoon. If I were a product, I'd be sold at a loss with no returns allowed.

Chapter 3

Grandma greeted me at our front door with a smile.

I was happy to see her. I was even happier to smell something delicious. "Did you make your famous caramel brownies?"

"Is that all you notice? The smell of sweets from the oven? What about my new dress?"

I looked her over to be polite. She wore a silky, lavender knee-length dress. I took her word that it was new. She is always buying new clothes. Unfortunately, she is always buying things for me, too. It wouldn't have been too bad if she bought me T-shirts or jeans, which I actually wore, instead of the frilly, lacy, pastel dresses and skirts she always insisted would look darling on me.

Ooh, that aroma was yummy. I needed to butter up Grandma ASAP so I could have a big serving of whatever tasty treat was in the oven. "Your dress is beautiful," I told Grandma before flashing her what I hoped was a darling smile. She is a big fan of darling things. "So what did you make today?"

"My famous M&M cookies."

"Mmm. You're the greatest." Who needed an ice cream parlor when there was a first-rate baker at home?

Grandma wiped her hands on her apron and walked with me toward the kitchen. "It's good to see you," she said. "Not your shoes, though. When are you going to get rid of those dirty things?"

I glanced down at my sneakers. True, they hadn't been white in a long time. They are mostly gray with black scuff marks and a few grass stains. But they are comfortable and good for running around and practicing karate moves. "Grandma, just because something's old, doesn't mean we just get rid of it."

She laughed. "I know what you're getting at. But don't call me old. I'm mature. And I don't walk around with gray hair. I dye it. So you shouldn't walk around with gray sneakers."

Grandma does look good. She should, with all the effort she spends on her appearance. For instance, I'd never seen her in sneakers. I doubt she even owned a pair. She wears high-heeled boots in the winter, sleek pumps in the fall and spring, and delicate sandals that show off her pretty, pink pedicured toenails in the summer. And you'd never know her hair was really gray. She dyes it black and Zena expertly styles it for her every Monday after school.

Grandma was the one who had introduced me to Zena. Since then, I'd been going to her every other weekend for years. Grandma likes how she handles hair. I like how she handles people, namely me. I can always talk to Zena about anything: my family, school, even Bud Bloom. And she does make my hair look good. Zena lets me pick whatever style I want from her big book. Sometimes we just improvise.

Of course, that's when Grandma usually says my hairstyle is too wild or, more precisely, "loud as a Las Vegas revue." I once asked Grandma how she knew about Las Vegas revues, since she also once said she wouldn't set foot in Sin City if it were the last place on Earth. She replied that she didn't need to eat the rotten apple to know it was poisonous. Admittedly, there have been times when my hair is on the loud side—like when Zena put temporary fiery red dye in it in honor of Valentine's Day, or a few years ago when she wove in

Pippi Longstocking extensions after I'd read the book. But I thought it was fun.

Speaking of fun, Tiffany ran into the kitchen, yelling, "Maya! All right, you're home!"

Grandma told Tiffany to lower her voice. I winked at my little sister as we ate Grandma's famous M&M cookies on plates covered with paper lace doilies. People who came over were always impressed by the doilies. Grandma said it was the extra touches that turn a house into a home. That philosophy was fine with me, as long as she was doing the extra touching. Not me. I had more important things to do, like hang with Tiffany.

"I'm so glad you're home," Tiffany exclaimed.

My sister always cheers me up. When we are together after school, I don't have to worry about homework or the Brain Bowl or Bud. I can just have fun. And I have to admit, I do like being with someone who practically worships me.

"I'm going to run for second-grade president!" squealed Tiffany.

"Great! What does the job entail?" I asked her.

"Entail? It's not an animal. No tails or anything."

I held back a snicker.

"Second-grade president gets to pick the line leader each week, make sure the whiteboard erasers and trash monitors are doing their jobs, and help the substitute when the teacher is gone."

"High five on that."

Before we could even raise our hands all the way up, Grandma stepped between us. "Be careful not to spill any crumbs," she said. "I don't like you getting wild at the kitchen table."

I tried not to roll my eyes. "You want help with your campaign?" I asked Tiffany.

"Sure. What's a campaign? Is that the stuff Mom drinks on New Year's Eve that we aren't supposed to touch?"

I laughed, and then explained to her about campaigning. I couldn't resist telling her about the 1800 presidential campaign. "Did you know John Adams lost his second campaign for president to Thomas Jefferson?" I'd just been studying that the night before. My own Brain Bowl teammates didn't seem interested in important facts. At least Tiffany listened to me.

After we cleared our plates and put them in the dishwasher, we headed toward the backyard to practice karate moves. Tiffany had started six months ago and was a yellow belt. She has a lot of potential.

As we made our way to the back door, I couldn't resist showing her a new move I'd learned the day before, a jumping, spinning back kick. "You have to jump quickly at the correct angle and spin just before kicking your leg really straight and high. It's definitely an advanced move." I jumped, spun a little too quickly, and kicked. "Keeyah!"

Oh no! My foot had caught on something against the wall. I heard a loud, high-pitched, terrifying noise nearby. It sounded almost like shattering glass.

Yikes! It *was* shattering glass. Not mere glass. The glass over Mom's law school diploma. Her diploma had been hanging on the hallway wall as long as I could remember, reminding our family and guests of Mom's accomplishments. But no more. Glass shards lay all over the floor, with the parchment paper resting on top of them.

Then I heard an even more terrifying sound: Grandma's heels clipping the hardwood floor at a fast pace. Then I heard her gasp.

I couldn't even look at her. I knew she was thinking what a bad person I was. "I'm really sorry," I said, as I stared down at the glass shards. "I'll pick up all the mess."

"Maya," Grandma said, "you are wilder than a busload of juvenile delinquents at one of those heavy metal concerts."

"How do you know about heavy metal concerts, Grandma?" Tiffany asked.

"Shh, Tiffany!" I shook my head at her, and then stared at the floor again.

"I am disappointed in you," Grandma continued. "And your mother will be devastated when she gets home and finds her diploma off the wall and full of glass. You need to start acting like a lady instead of a frog on caffeine."

"What's caffeine?" Tiffany asked.

I shushed her. It wasn't the time to explain that caffeine was an ingredient in coffee, cola, and even chocolate, and some anthropologists had dated its use back to the Stone Age. With Grandma glaring at me, it was a time to keep my big mouth shut. I knew she was even more disappointed in me than usual.

I should act more ladylike, I told myself. It wasn't just the glass around Mom's diploma I'd messed up today. I'd messed up everything. Everything. I had embarrassed myself and Bud when I put him into a hammerlock. I had nagged my teammates to study. And I had refused to go to Baskin-Robbins with them. And to top it all off, I had ruined my mother's diploma.

I blinked back tears and told Grandma that I'd get the broom.

"It was just an accident," Tiffany said. "I'll help you sweep up."

I swiped at my eyes. A few tears had managed to escape. "Tiffany, please, just get out of here. You're not old enough to help. The last thing I need is for you to impale yourself with glass shards."

"What's *impale?*" Tiffany asked.

"Not now," I said. "Just leave me alone, okay?"

She ran into her room.

I told myself I'd follow her to make sure she was okay just as soon as I cleaned up the mess on the floor.

I was still sweeping when Mom came home. She looked exhausted, as usual: her shoulders were slumped under her gray suit, one hand was loaded with her laptop, and the other held a leather bag full of documents. She had been working like crazy preparing for a big upcoming trial. After I explained what had happened and apologized four times, she stared at the dustpan full of glass, shook her head, and walked down the hallway.

I sort of wished she would yell at me. For the past few months she had been ignoring almost everything— me included— in favor of her work. I was getting mighty tired of it. She did sigh at dinnertime when Grandma went into one of her riffs about how irresponsible I was.

But it was a quick sigh on her way to the den to finish up a few phone calls. Those must have been long calls. She was still in the den when I went to bed.

I turned off my bedside lamp and closed my eyes. It was dark in my room, but my brain was lit up like neon. What a day it had been. I tried to get to sleep, but I just couldn't stop thinking. I couldn't remember who was president between Millard Filmore and James Buchanan, or the capital of South Dakota. I wondered if our team should study more sports topics, since none of us were strong in that area. Mostly, I kept thinking about all the accidents I had caused, the major nagging I did, and Bud's smile, which flashed especially bright and wide when he chatted with Lindsey.

Argh! That smile! I needed to empty out my brain of Bud thoughts ASAP. I would never get to sleep while thinking of him. I needed a major distraction.

There was only one thing to do. I tiptoed into the living room, which was now dark and a bit creepy, turned on a lamp, and switched on the TV. I scrolled through the list of our recorded shows and selected my favorite, *Full House*.

I pretend I only record it for Tiffany's sake, but I am the one with the secret passion for the show. *Secret,* because I know *Full House* is a waste of time, and I am known for not wasting time. I hardly ever watch TV, unless it is a Discovery channel show about something I could be tested on during the Brain Bowl. *Passion,* for unknown reasons. I'm not sure if it is the cuteness of the Olsen twins, the hunkiness of Jessie, or the funniness of Kimmie, but *Full House* always cheers me up.

As usual, the last scene showed the three sisters in a group hug. I couldn't help noticing how nicely the girls dressed and how adorable they were. None of them even wore sneakers. In real life, Mary-Kate and Ashley are women, multimillionaires, and still adorable. I'm not sure what happened to the other actresses on the show, but I assume they are still adorable too. I bet none of them memorizes facts every day or practices dangerous karate moves. And I am sure they never put guys in hammerlocks or wear stained shirts and old sneakers. Heck, in every magazine photo the Olsens wear full-on makeup, trendy clothes, and a whole bunch of accessories. I am lucky if I remember to put on earrings.

I knew Grandma would be happy if I were more ladylike like them. Maybe Bud would even flirt with me like he did with Lindsey. And ladylike girls wouldn't damage their mother's diploma, even if it were an accident.

I decided right then that I was going to change.

I clicked off the TV, found a pen and notepad, and began writing out a plan. Starting at that moment, at 1:17 a.m., I was going to become perfectly ladylike.

I, Maya Truitt, would make myself over.

Chapter 4

I woke up at 8:33 a.m. I couldn't believe how late I had slept. What a waste of time. I usually studied for the Brain Bowl every weekend morning from seven to eight o'clock. Oversleeping threw off my entire schedule.

I yawned. If it was so late, why was I still tired? Then I remembered getting up, watching *Full House,* and formulating a new plan to become ladylike. I had even written down the steps I would take. I rubbed my eyes, retrieved the list from my nightstand, and looked it over.

One: Wear makeup every day.

Man, I must have been really out of it this morning. I never wore makeup. But most girls at school did. Grandma always says true ladies are never seen without their faces on. I pictured Lindsey's pretty, shiny face and pink lips and decided to buy some makeup right away.

Two: Lose the jeans and T-shirts.

If I didn't wear my jeans and T-shirts, what in the world could I wear? I had my church clothes, and the dresses and skirts Grandma had given me. Last week, the minister had told Mom how pretty I looked. Maybe Bud would think I looked pretty too. I decided to give it a try.

Three: Wear feminine hairstyles.

That one won't be too hard, I told myself. Zena will probably relish trying out new, mature and demure hairdos on me.

Four: Don't play rough anymore.

No objection to that rule. It wasn't smart to play rough, considering my Bud-wrangling, diploma-ruining disasters. Showing off karate moves, even to my little sister, was just plain unladylike. No matter how much fun it was, I knew it could cause serious damage.

Five: Don't be so bossy.

I didn't want to be called a drill sergeant ever again. If my teammates decided to chat or go out for ice cream, I would no longer be the one who argued against it. Maybe we could win the Brain Bowl without studying so much, I told myself, and tried really hard to believe it.

Six: Flirt.

If I wanted Bud Bloom to see me as a love interest, I would have to play the part. I wasn't sure how to flirt, having never done so, but maybe I could research it. I wondered if there was a good instructional site on the Net. Or perhaps the library carried a how-to book on flirting that I could quietly check out. I knew a little about flirting, having observed other girls in high school. Basically, it seemed to involve exaggerated forms of giggling, hair-shaking, and eyelash-batting. I'd probably have to practice a bit in front of a mirror. Perhaps I could work out a practice schedule, such as three times a day for eight minutes at a time.

Seven: Accept social invitations, even if they cut into study time or Tiffany time.

This rule was crucial. If I had gone to Baskin-Robbins, for instance, maybe Bud would have seen me as more than just a drill sergeant and maybe Mom's diploma would have stayed intact.

I stared at my written plan and tried not to frown. There were *only* seven rules. Some of them weren't even that harsh. I can do it, I told myself. I can change. Grandma will be so proud. And Tiffany will look up to me even more, and I might get more of Mom's attention too. Also, I bet I'll fit right in at school, and Bud Bloom might even finally realize that I'm the love of his life.

I jumped out of bed, determined to execute my plan immediately. This weekend would be spent in preparation, and on Monday I'd go to school as the new me. I could hardly wait.

The first thing I did was to find the pink bathrobe Grandma had given me for my birthday. The color wasn't so bad, if one was a fan of, say, bubble gum, or if one was under ten years of age. The word *Princess* appeared all over the robe's fabric. The old Maya would rather be president or prime minister than princess. In fact, she thought there were hundreds of jobs preferable to a princess gig. But the new Maya felt that wearing the princess bathrobe was the first step toward her wonderful new life.

I tried not to shiver as I pulled the pink robe over my navy blue pajamas.

Grandma smiled like crazy when she saw me come into the dining room. As I removed a hard white block of sleep goo from the corner of my eye, she told me I looked just like Halle Berry when she won her Academy Award.

"March 2002," I couldn't help adding. I thought Grandma was getting a little carried away. I hadn't even brushed my hair or teeth yet. Wait until she saw me wearing makeup. She'd probably jump up and down like our school cheerleaders did at a pep rally.

Grandma's mention of the Academy Awards reminded me that I needed to study that subject more. Breakfast wasn't ready and my family was busy, so I had a little time for Brain Bowl prep. While Tiffany whipped up the pancake batter, Mom rifled through the legal documents she had brought home the night before, and Grandma read the home improvement section of the paper, I made a chronological list of all the Oscar-winning movies from memory and then checked it against the list in my notebook.

Yes! I'd gotten them all correct. Maybe it would be a better day than the day before. It couldn't get much worse.

I waited until we were enjoying Grandma and Tiffany's heart-shaped blueberry pancakes before asking my mom if she'd buy me some makeup.

Tiffany laughed so hard the orange juice she was drinking came out of her nose, which was not a pretty sight. "Good one, Maya," she said. "Next you'll be asking for a new dress."

I glared at her. "I may have said in the past that I didn't care for makeup or nice clothes—"

"You said you'd rather die than spend time putting criminal glop on your face."

I shook my head. "Not criminal, Tiffany. Chemical."

"It's still glop. That's what you said."

Mom looked up from her legal papers. "You don't need makeup on that pretty face of yours, Maya. You're only fourteen. You're still my baby."

I couldn't help rolling my eyes. "Fourteen does not equate to babyhood. In some countries, that's the age girls become mothers."

"You want to have children now too?" Mom asked.

Tiffany shook her head. "Maya said parenthood is for people with nothing else going on in their lives."

My mom glared at me. In turn, I glared at Tiffany. Insulting Mom would not encourage her to open her wallet.

"Why are you acting so goofy?" Tiffany asked. "It's like that time that guy Bud came over to study and you forgot my name when you were trying to introduce us."

Grandma took a dainty sip of her juice. No orange juice ever exploded out of Grandma's nose that was for sure. "I think it's terrific that Maya is finally showing signs of caring about her appearance. Maybe she'll even start wearing that perfume I bought her on Valentine's Day."

"If you want to wear makeup— tastefully, that is— you can," Mom told me. "But you can use your allowance money."

I slumped my shoulders. "All right. But who's going to drive me to the store?"

"Ooh, let me!" Grandma shouted like I'd just asked who wanted to drive me to the Ritz Carlton to dine with Denzel Washington. "I can help you pick out the perfect makeup for your face. Let's see. You have a heart-shaped face, so you'll need some powder on your chin to make it look wider, and some mauve lipstick for your coloring, and bronze shadows for your eyes. We'll blend three colors together, of course, for your eyelids. You should also buy some cover-up for those days when you get blemishes. Let's face it, Maya, you're a teen and you do come down with a little acne now and again."

"Grandma," I protested.

Tiffany giggled. Fortunately, she wasn't drinking anything at the time.

In her enthusiasm for my new, ladylike aspirations, Grandma ignored us both. "We'll go to Saks. That's Saks Fifth Avenue, for the uninitiated." She winked at me.

I sighed as hard as I could. "If I'm spending my own money, I'll have to buy drugstore makeup." I shook my head for more sympathy points. "And not very much makeup either." I stretched my lower lip into a pout to amass bonus points.

Grandma beamed at me. "Let me buy it for you. A birthday gift."

I beamed right back at her.

"Maya's birthday was three months ago," Mom said. "You already bought her a gift. The new dress."

What a killjoy. If I had access to a mirror at that moment, I bet I would have seen my face fall at least three and a half inches.

"It was generous of you to offer," Mom told Grandma. "But I'd rather have Maya buy her own makeup. That's what her allowance is for."

Actually, I was hoping to use my allowance for other stuff. Fun stuff. Tiffany and I were saving up for a karaoke set, and I wanted the new Dungeons and Dragons book and tickets for a karate tournament. Some of the most famous black belts in the world were coming to my town, and seats cost twenty-six dollars for a full day sure to be thrilling. I'd hate to miss the tournament because I had to get mascara and lipstick.

I pleaded with Mom. "Grandma's a beauty expert, and she wants to buy me quality products. I bet Saks Fifth Avenue has much better makeup than I could afford, and did you know that makeup has been around since approximately 4000 BC? The Egyptians used it first." I couldn't help sharing my knowledge of facts I found fascinating.

"Maya," Mom said. "If you're mature enough to put makeup on your face, then you should be mature enough to pay for it."

"But—"

"End of discussion."

Sigh. There was no use arguing with Mom, anyway. She argued for a living, and she was quite good at it too. Last year, she was even written about in *Middletown Magazine* as one of the top ten female lawyers in our town.

"In fact," Mom continued, "I wish I could talk you out of wearing makeup at your age. But I've got two hundred and eighty pages of declarations and interrogatories to bone up on this weekend."

"Mom, you said you'd play Frisbee with me," Tiffany said.

"Just for a few minutes, okay? After the trial, things will be a lot easier."

We'd been hearing that a lot from her over the last couple of months. But I didn't say anything. Last time I quoted the all work and no play line, Tiffany said that I worked too hard also.

"At least Maya will play with me," Tiffany said.

"Maybe. But first I have to go shopping and sort through my closet and practice some stuff."

Tiffany probably assumed I meant practicing for the Brain Bowl. I would let her assume that, because what I really planned to do was embarrassing. I needed to look in the mirror and make sure I could bat my eyelashes and smile in a sultry way. Once I got that down, I would attempt to eyelash-bat and smile sultrily while simultaneously giggling or talking or both. Lindsey Jacques probably could do it in her sleep.

"Everyone's too busy for me," Tiffany whined.

I shrugged. "Sorry." I really was sorry. Usually we spend a lot of time hanging together on the weekends. I could see why Tiffany was a little upset. "Hey, you want to try on some of my new makeup, after I get it?"

"Ugh. No. I'd rather eat entails."

"Entrails, you mean. The insides of animals."

"Well, sorry if I'm just not phisticated enough for you," she said. "But I have no desire to put on makeup."

She looked so upset I didn't even tell her the correct word was *sophisticated*. I cleared my throat. "Who can drive me to the drugstore?"

Approximately an hour and forty-three minutes later, Grandma and I pulled into our driveway.

"I'm glad you're finally starting to care about your appearance like a young lady should," Grandma said.

I thanked Grandma for the ride and then rushed out of the car. I could get in an hour of karate and Brain Bowl practice before my appointment with Zena. I really needed to work on my front ball kick–back fist combination, as well as study chemical abbreviations.

"Maya," Grandma called after me. "Let me show you how to put on your face."

Ugh. I supposed I needed to practice that too. I wanted my makeup done right for school on Monday. But I didn't want an old person telling me how to apply my new stuff. I couldn't run the risk of appearing out-of-date. "I'll do it myself," I told Grandma. "It has to be easier than memorizing Nobel Prize winners from the last twenty years. Thanks, anyway."

I quickly realized learning the list of prizewinners was simple compared to putting on makeup. I never thought makeup application could be so difficult. For instance, the blush I bought barely showed up on my dark cheeks. I had to cake it on to make my face red. The mascara got all clumpy. And the lipstick seemed too bright. I wanted the appearance of full lips, not blimp lips. But after just one coating of Luscious Liplock I resembled Mick Jagger, if he were forty years younger, black, and female. As I stared at my bright countenance in the bathroom mirror, I decided the colorful look was probably better than my usual plain-faced look. It was just a matter of getting used to it.

Tiffany sure seemed to have a hard time getting used to my new appearance. After staring and staring at me, she finally said I looked weird.

I told her she just wasn't old enough to appreciate my womanly appearance. Then I left the house. I biked over to Zena's shop because it was only a mile from our house. Also riding my bike gave me a good excuse not to wear a dress. A part of me—a huge part of me—was relieved to wear my sweatshirt and jeans. It was hard enough adjusting to the makeup. I didn't have it in me to transition to girly clothes too.

Zena obviously had an even harder time adjusting to the makeup than I did. She went over to greet me as I walked into the store but then stopped short and planted her feet on the ground like she couldn't move.

Her smile started to form as I moved closer. When I was about two feet from her, the chuckles came. When I was only inches away, she lost control, laughing so hard she not only couldn't walk, she could hardly stand. She leaned over, her big hands square on her plump knees, laughing loud as you please while everyone in the beauty shop stared at me. Well, not the lady in the back getting her hair washed, or the tiny girl getting cornrows, who kept moving around while poor Rayshawnda stood behind her and told her to hold still. But everyone else's eyes were fixed on me.

I, of course, just wanted to die right there on the spot. I bet Zena would have felt majorly guilty about killing one of her best customers, not to mention a friend. And a death in the beauty shop would not be good for business.

Fortunately, I didn't die. I didn't even collapse into a coma or faint. Though I did find it a little hard to breathe. I stood in front of Zena and shook my head.

She covered her mouth and kept trying to stop laughing, only to bust out in giggles or chuckles after a few seconds. Finally, on about the eighth attempt, she stopped. She put her hands on her hips. "Fantastic joke, Maya."

I glared at her. "What joke?"

"Hey, I know it's April Fool's Day today. I already played a trick on my husband. I pretended I wanted to quit the hairstyling business. He didn't believe me for one second. He knows how I love this job. But your face." She pointed at me and shook her head. "That is classic. That the best April Fool's Day stunt I seen in a lo-o-o-o-ng time. You do that yourself?"

I put my hands on my hips just like Zena was doing. I was starting to get mad. "This is my new look."

She laughed again. "You good, girl." She pointed at my cheeks. "How much face gunk you waste to pull that off?"

I shook my head. "I guess I need more practice with makeup."

"Oh no. No, no, no. You ain't serious, baby, are you? What you doing putting makeup on that gorgeous young face of yours?"

"You think it looks that bad?" My voice cracked a little when I said it.

She gave me a hug, right in the middle of the beauty parlor. That is one thing about Zena, she doesn't care who is around watching or listening. She just does what she wants, no matter what other people think.

I cared, though. I shut my eyes so I wouldn't see everyone staring at me, and gave her a little hug back.

"You don't need no makeup," she said, still gripping me in her large, soft arms. "But if you going to wear it, you got to tone it down. Way down. Wa-a-y down." She fingered the charm she always wore around her neck, a silver Z dangling from a silver chain.

I knew she played with that charm when she was deep in thought, right before she said something important. Or sometimes when she was about to talk, she'd play with that charm of hers, and then clamp her lips right up. She once told me that the most under-valued skill a person could have was being a good listener. She said that with so many talkers running off their mouths in the world, it was always easy to find practice.

It seemed like Zena was getting ready to use her listening skills on me. She said, "You tell me how you'd like that pretty hair of yours today, and then we two will have us a long conversation about what's going on. Zena's going to help you through what it is you're going through. 'Cause, baby, I know you must be going through something. Something hard, that might be too big for one person to figure out, no matter how smart that girl is."

I stared at my sneakers. "Yesterday, I almost killed Bud Bloom."

"That nice boy from the Brain Bowl? You two love-birds get in a fight?"

"We're not lovebirds. I don't even think we're like-birds at this point. To him, I'm just the drill sergeant who tries to boss him around."

"So you trying to be less bossy? More girly-like?"

"You got it, Zena."

"If he don't like you for who you is, he's a fool. And what do you want with a fool?"

"He's the cutest, funniest, smartest fool I know. That's what I want."

She sighed. "I'm sorry, honey, for laughing at your face. Stubborn girl like you ain't going to listen to me, no matter how right I am. And you know I'm right, girl."

I smiled at her. "I guess I have to find out for myself that you're right." Since Zena was being understanding about my new look, I told her that I wanted something sweet, low-key, and delicate for my new hairstyle.

She swung her head back and forth. I knew what she was thinking: *No, no, and a thousand times no.* But she bit her lip so she wouldn't say anything and started shaking her head slower. She rubbed the silver *Z* like it was a twig and she was desperate for fire. After a while she stopped her head-shaking and charm-rubbing altogether. She calmed down and smiled at me in a phony way that looked like she was consciously ordering her lips to move up.

"Every young person, she got to find herself," she said. "And I don't especially like the path you're taking, but I suppose it's a path that's got to be took."

So I got my hair straightened for the first time in my life, and Zena didn't complain about it. Though I did catch her reflection in the mirror, shaking her head every so often. Then Zena put my hair in a flip just like I asked for.

"If I didn't know you better," she told me as she brushed stray hairs off of my T-shirt, "I'd think you were one of them dainty, delicate kinds of girls. Like one of them princesses in a Disney movie waiting for a prince to save her, only a lot darker than most of the princesses in the movies and with a lot more stuff on her face."

I laughed out of the sheer joy of being compared to a princess character. That was just what I'd been shooting for. That, or the Lindsey Jacques look, which, come to think of it, was a princess look anyway.

Bud will never call me a drill sergeant now.

Chapter 5

I had to wake up a half hour earlier on Monday to accommodate my brow alignment, makeup, and ironing. Beauty demands sacrifice, I told myself as I tweezed my eyebrows and tried not to scream.

I put on my church dress, which Grandma had bought for me a few months ago. I usually hated the dress, with its yellow gauze that made my skin feel itchy, and the small white polka dots that reminded me of bird droppings. I only wore it to church and only because Mom made me.

But it was the perfect choice for my new look.

My plan was to undo the top two buttons when I got to school so I'd look more like Brandi and less like Condoleeza Rice. I respected Ms. Rice's intelligence and hard work, but I didn't think she was exactly the type of feminine ideal I was going for. On the other hand, I didn't want to lean toward a harsh Janet Jackson look or even the somewhat wild wardrobe of Beyoncé. Luckily, unbuttoning the top of my dress would relieve my neck itch. If only I could find a way to stop the makeup from making my face itch.

I wore my flats, but planned to change into my mom's special-occasion shoes that were hidden in my backpack. Mom's shoes were a size bigger than what I usually wore, but I figured they'd have to do. I didn't own any high heels, personally. Not yet. But shopping was part of my plan.

Of course, I also wore my new makeup. At Zena's suggestion, it was toned down from Saturday, at least on my cheeks. I put on only five coats of blush this morning, instead of the eight I had used before.

All those preparations left me no time for a regular breakfast, so I headed for the kitchen to down a glass of orange juice. When I passed the dining room table, Grandma told me to stop. "Twirl around," she ordered. As I modeled my new look for her, her face seemed to brighten as much as my rouged cheeks, and she nodded her head up and down. She said, "Aren't you the lovely one?" about five times.

Mom sat at the table too, staring at some notes she'd scribbled on a yellow legal pad. I asked her what she thought of the new me. She glanced up, said, "Lovely, dear," and then wrote something on the margin of her paper. She probably would have responded the same way if I were wearing a gorilla suit.

"I think you look like a clown," Tiffany protested.

I patted her head. She was too young to understand about makeup and other womanly things.

She said, "Give me a break, Clownhead."

So I stuck out my tongue at her.

At school, the response to the new me fell somewhere in the middle of Grandma's, Mom's, and Tiffany's reactions. Though no one was as enthusiastic as Grandma, most people paid me more attention than Mom had this morning, and everyone seemed more accepting than Tiffany had been. Nobody called me Clownhead, at least not to my face.

The best reaction came from the one person I hadn't expected to even notice me. Near the end of history class, Lindsey Jacques (!) leaned over her desk and whispered, "You look divine."

It was only the first day of my plan, and already one of the prettiest, most popular freshman had given me a compliment. I couldn't help flashing her a humongous smile.

I also couldn't help worrying whether I had lipstick on my teeth. That gunk had made an ugly red mark on my juice glass this morning. As I smiled, I curled my lips over my teeth, just in case.

Lindsey asked if I was okay.

I put my hand over my mouth and nodded. Oh no. I hoped there wasn't lipstick on my hand now. I also hoped the bell would ring ASAP.

The big test of my new look was, of course, Brain Bowl practice. I forced myself not to rush to Mr. Beebe's classroom after school like I usually did. For one thing, speed-walking wasn't ladylike. For another, I had on Mom's high heels, and I knew that falling on my face wasn't ladylike either.

I was still the first one there. What the heck were my teammates doing after the final bell rang? Making small talk or something? I decided I should do that too. I made a mental note to add *Practice small talk* to my plan.

Then I thought, I might as well practice on Mr. Beebe, since he's awake for once. He was staring at his laptop.

I greeted him with a friendly, "Hey, Mr. Beebe."

He grunted something in return, keeping his gaze on the laptop monitor.

"You think we'll get rain today?"

He wrinkled his forehead. "He's going to shoot the moon."

"Huh? Who? A psychopath or something is trying to shoot the moon? Was something about the moon in the weather forecast?"

He glanced at me and put his fingers on his lips. "Shh. I'm playing hearts on the Internet. If troglypop14 shoots the moon, I get twenty-six points and the game is over. You don't need anything, do you?"

Just some small talk practice, I thought. Obviously I wasn't going to get it with Mr. Beebe.

Luckily, the team started arriving. First, Daisy and Rani strolled in, chatting. I knew they weren't thinking what I was thinking: that the championship game was only three weeks away and if we didn't start pulling together soon we didn't stand a chance. They were talking about reality TV shows.

Because I didn't want to be called a drill sergeant again, I tried to join in their conversation. "I saw *Survivor*," I said.

"The season that ended a few months ago?" Daisy asked. "Oh, wow, you look . . . different."

"Why the new look?" Rani asked.

Because my old look was pathetic and getting me nowhere in life. Though I thought it, I didn't say it aloud. Instead, I focused on the goal at hand: small talk.

"I saw an episode of *Survivor* two years ago. Or possibly three years ago. Interesting show. Did you know many of the islands in the South Pacific have a history of military occupation in World War II? Ooh, we should try to memorize their names in case it comes up at competition."

"You want us to study now," Daisy said. "We get the message."

Oh no. I had failed at small talk. How had it devolved so quickly into nag talk? I tried to recover. "Let's wait until everyone gets here. So, um, what's *American Idol* about?"

"You don't know?" Daisy asked, like I'd just questioned whether the earth revolved around the sun or what CO_2 stood for.

I bit my lip. "I know *American Idol* is a reality show. People try out for it, right? And there's a mean guy on it or something? Simon Scowl?"

Daisy laughed. "Simon Cowell. It's on, like, three nights a week."

Then they started talking about this supposedly totally cute guy who got voted off last week. I stood next to them, trying to look interested and trying not to look at my watch to figure out how much time we were wasting by not studying.

When Bud and Dirk sauntered in, I put my palm over my watch so I couldn't calculate exactly how late they were. Then I spied the clock on the classroom wall and based my calculations on that. It was hard to change old habits. I couldn't help realizing that we could have had fourteen additional minutes for studying if everyone had hurried over after school.

But at least I didn't make a stink about it. The old Maya would have clapped her hands to get everyone's attention, complained about the latecomers, and said, "Let's study the English poets. I heard there were three questions on them last year. Get out your pens and paper." The new Maya excused herself from Daisy and Rani, walked over to the guys, and smiled like a head cheerleader.

"Whoa, man, you're wearing a dress," Dirk said. "Wild."

Bud scratched his head. "You look different."

Different-good or different-bad? I wanted to ask him. But that would have seemed too neurotic. So I just kept smiling and said, "Do you think we'll get rain today?"

My attempt at small talk was not only lame, it also made Dirk go outside to check the clouds. Small talk was not supposed to drive people out of the room. Sigh.

It also made me want to give Bud a pop quiz on the different kinds of clouds. But that was just the sort of thing the old Maya would have done.

Instead, while Dirk was outside, I batted my eyelashes at Bud and told him I liked his shirt. I added, "An awful lot." Then I explained I meant *awful* in a good way, not in a bad way, such as if his shirt were awful. "Because it's not. Awful."

Yikes. What the heck was coming out of my mouth? And I had forgotten to keep up the eyelash-blinking. I batted them rapidly to make up for lost time. My eyelids were getting really tired.

"Is there something in your eye?" Bud asked.

I put a kibosh on the blinking. "Um, no."

Then I had a horrifying thought: What if all that lash-batting gave me raccoon eyes? I asked Bud if my mascara was running. "It's supposed to be waterproof," I informed him.

Oh, sheesh. I didn't think guys were interested in talking about runny mascara. In fact, it probably grossed them out. I needed major help in the flirting department. If flirting were a subject tested on the Brain Bowl, I would lose for sure.

Dirk returned to the classroom and gave a full report on possible weather conditions. I found it a lot more interesting than talking about waterproof mascara, but Bud looked bored.

Making small talk was a lot harder than I thought, or at least making small talk that was interesting, anyway. Was small talk supposed to be interesting? Maybe not, and maybe by its very definition. If it were interesting, it might be called large talk, or at least medium talk.

"Maya!" Rani shouted. "Don't you see what time it is?" She pointed to the clock. "Why didn't you tell us how late it was and get us moving?"

I forced myself to shrug. "That's really the job of the faculty advisor."

We all turned to Mr. Beebe. He was hunched over his laptop, grumbling, "Why can't these blockheads cover their passes?"

"You okay, Mr. Beebe?" Rani asked.

He looked up, startled, as if he hadn't realized anyone else was in the classroom. "When you play hearts, you need to cover your passes or people will shoot the moon. I've lost four games in a row. But it's not my fault. I've been playing with blockheads." He stared at the laptop again.

"Wow," Daisy said. "That's the most Mr. Beebe has ever spoken to us."

"I miss Mrs. Bennett," Rani said.

That got us talking about our old faculty advisor and her new baby while I made surreptitious checks of my watch.

By the time Dirk did a wolf whistle and said we absolutely had to start practicing for the Brain Bowl, I'd been in the classroom over an hour and my teammates had been there for forty-eight minutes. Supposing that we could learn ninety facts an hour, and that 10 percent of those facts might be remembered later on, the hour spent dawdling and chitchatting caused our team to lose the potential of forty-five facts (nine facts multiplied by five people) memorized correctly for the Brain Bowl.

Wait. That was the old Maya's way of thinking. I reminded myself that I had socialized like I had wanted. The new Maya found great value in improving social skills. Socializing was supposed to make a person happy and lead to better health. Statistically speaking, people with friends lived significantly longer than those without.

Though if living longer meant spending significantly more time making small talk, I wasn't sure socializing was worth it. Plus, I really, really did not want to lose the Brain Bowl.

Chapter 6

The first thing I did when I got home from school was check my reflection in the bathroom mirror. On my left side, my clumped mascara made it appear as if I had three giant lashes. On my right side, my mascara had trickled down under my eye, giving the impression that I'd run into a small spider web. Also, my lipstick had smeared on my front tooth and I had a pink rash on my neck from the gauze on my dress collar that had been itching me all day.

"You look weird." Tiffany had followed me into the bathroom.

"Thanks a lot," I said sarcastically, though I was happy to see her.

"I was waiting forever for you."

"We got started late at practice." I patted her head. She wore her hair in an adorable bunch of braids Zena had made.

I checked my reflection again. At least my straightened hair had held up.

"If I tell you that you look just like Beyond Me, will you play Frisbee with me?" Tiffany asked.

"Who?" Beyond Me was beyond me.

"You know, that singer from Desitin's Child."

I laughed. "Beyoncé from Destiny's Child. And they broke up. I wish I looked like Beyoncé."

"I bet she can't do half the karate moves you can, and you could beat her in a Brain Bowl challenge any day," Tiffany said.

"Thanks." I smiled at her. "Yeah, I'll play Frisbee with you."

I was just about to open the sliding glass door to the backyard when I thought of something. "Oh, geez," I told Tiffany. "I can't play Frisbee. I just filed and polished my nails last night. I had to use three coats of stuff, and it took me almost an hour. I don't want to chip my fingernails after all that work."

Tiffany furrowed her brow. "You promised."

"I'll do something else with you. A fun project I just remembered."

"You'll help me on my champagne for second-grade president?"

"Campaign. But, no. Actually, I was thinking of going through my closet to determine if I have any feminine and fashionable clothes to wear." I tried to make my voice enthusiastic, but it wasn't easy.

"That sounds lame," Tiffany said.

"You know, *lame* isn't a nice word. It's definitely not ladylike. You should rephrase that. Say something like 'I'd rather pass on your suggestion, but I appreciate the offer.'"

Tiffany rolled her eyes. "I don't 'preciate the offer. I don't 'preciate your stupid new plan. I would 'preciate your playing Frisbee with me or helping me with the election coming up so I don't come up with a lame champagne slogan."

I shook my head. "For one thing, the word is *appreciate*. And the other word is *campaign*. For another thing, if you're going to be so negative, you don't have to hang with me."

I opened my closet door. I had a lot of clothes to sort. "It's okay with me if you'd like to help, but I don't want to hear you complaining again."

Tiffany didn't answer, so I assumed she was being careful not to complain.

I started rifling through my rack of T-shirts. The first shirt bore a picture of Einstein, captioned "$e=mc^2$." It was one of my favorites, but wouldn't do for the new me. The next two T-shirts were from my martial arts studio. Nope. Karate screamed "old Maya." Next was a shirt I got last summer that said *Camp Lakota*. It was sort of feminine because it pictured a bright blue stream and a pretty mountain.

I took the camp shirt and its hanger off the rod and held it up. "What do you think of this one, Tiff?"

No response.

I turned around.

Tiffany had left the room.

I felt kind of guilty. After all, I had promised to help my sister with her campaign. I was so busy, though. I could at least help her create a slogan to center the campaign around.

Hadn't the school marquee suggested I come up with a slogan? Actually, it had said to make up a slogan for myself. But with my new beauty routines and social endeavors, I barely had time to create slogans for Tiffany, let alone for myself.

I leafed through the clothes hanging in my closet, wondering what my slogan would be now. Pretty and Petite? Dressed to Perfection? To be honest, it should be: Girl Whose Feet Are Killing Her.

I kicked off my mom's high heels and noticed blisters on both of my big toes. Being ladylike sure was hard work.

The phone rang, but I didn't leave my room. I figured Grandma would pick it up. She gets most of the telephone traffic anyway. She is always getting calls from her pinochle group, or her best friend Judy, or someone in her knitting circle.

When Grandma came into my bedroom with the phone and said Lindsey Jacques was on the line for me, I nearly died. What in the world was she doing calling me? "Are you sure?" I asked Grandma. "Lindsey Jacques from school?"

"I don't know if she's from your school or not," Grandma said, "but there's a sweet-sounding girl asking for you, who claims to be Lindsey Jacques."

I took the phone from Grandma, but in my eagerness I dropped it on the ground. I mouthed "sorry" as Grandma shook her head at me. I was barely able to rescue the phone and say "hello" into the mouthpiece. When Lindsey Jacques talked to me in school, I could hardly breathe. A personal phone call from her made my heart palpitate.

Holy mackerel! She invited me to a party. Not any old party either. Her birthday party! A slumber party!

My heart beat so loud and fast, I almost expected it to burst out of my chest. My new plan was working far better than I'd hoped.

"Of course I can make it to your party!" I gushed over the phone. "I'd love to go!"

Lindsey laughed. "I like your enthusiasm. But don't you want to know when it is? And shouldn't you check with your parents first?"

"Oh, yes, yes, of course. When is it?"

"It starts at four-thirty on April twenty-first."

"Hold on." I put my hand over the mouthpiece of the phone, walked out of my room, and asked Grandma, knowing she'd be delighted that I was going to the party for a "sweet-sounding girl."

"That's the night of the cocktail party for the opera fund-raiser," Grandma said. "You promised to watch Tiffany so your mother and I could attend."

"I have to babysit?"

"You promised. A lady never goes back on her word."

I bit my lip. This lady never got invited to a party by Lindsey Jacques before.

I was about to break the bad news to Lindsey when I realized how uncool that sounded. Girls with good social lives wouldn't be babysitting on a weekend night. Would they? No. They'd be going to a party, or several parties.

I took my hand off of the mouthpiece of the phone, and said, "I'm sorry. I'm busy until about eight with a prior social engagement."

"That's okay," Lindsey said. "Come over after. My party's going to last a long time. From four thirty in the afternoon until ten the next morning. I want to try to stay up all night."

"Cool!" I said.

"We'll be like zombies all day on April twenty-second."

"April twenty-second!" Oh no! That was the day of the Brain Bowl. I couldn't pull an all-nighter before the County Championship competition, unless it was to study.

"You sound kind of bummed," Lindsey said.

Try mega-bummed. But I couldn't tell her that. If I told Lindsey why I couldn't go to her party, she'd think I was a total nerd.

"Maya? Are you still there?"

I cleared my throat. "Uh, yeah. Your party sounds, uh, neat. I mean, awesome."

"It is definitely going to be awesome. I'm planning a really cool dance contest, and everyone's supposed to bring their best makeup and perfume and three of their favorite outfits to show off. How awesome is that?"

I was glad she meant that as a rhetorical question. Because on a scale of one to ten on the awesome spectrum—one being lowest and ten being highest— I'd have to give it a zero, or perhaps a negative number if that was allowed. A party centered on wearing fancy clothes and makeup sounded a lot less than awesome to me.

"Maya?"

"Oh, yeah. Um, your party seems totally, um, awesome. I'll be there," I told Lindsey.

"Excellent!" she gushed.

"Excellent," I moaned.

After the phone call, I paced my bedroom, wondering how I could get out of Lindsey's party without hurting her feelings. Because besides being popular and pretty, she seemed nice too. I opened the drawer in my nightstand and took out the written plan I'd made. Number seven said as clear as Newton's theory of gravity, "Accept social invitations."

I guess I had to go to the sleepover. I sighed. So much for winning the Brain Bowl championship this year.

Chapter 7

I had been right about Lindsey Jacques. She was a nice girl. We started hanging out more and more. She even gave me a lipstick, along with advice on makeup. She told me one coating of rouge was plenty, instead of the five I'd been wearing. That's what my mother had said, but it's hard to take beauty advice from someone who wears glasses and flats, and would rather read *American Lawyer* than *Cosmo Girl*. Lindsey Jacques not only reads *Cosmo Girl,* she is a subscriber.

If only measured by how much my looks had improved, my plan would be judged a success. After getting up a half hour early every day to put on my face, iron my clothes, and tinker with my nails, I had earned the right to look better. If the number of times

I had tripped in my mother's high heels were taken into account, my plan would be judged a disaster. If my plan were measured in how happy I had become, my plan had succeeded. I sure was smiling a lot. In public, anyway. When I remembered.

And I was getting better at being a lady. I remembered not to rub my eyes, no matter how tired I was, so I wouldn't have raccoon-face. And the new me wasn't spending time on karate practice. So what if I missed that part of my life? And the awful feeling that my team was going to bomb at the Brain Bowl was probably just nerves. Feminine girls like me had more important concerns.

At the practice on Thursday, exactly sixty-eight hours before the County Championship game, the Brain Bowl was the number one thing on my mind. Well, apart from Bud Bloom.

Mr. Beebe made the new me miserable. But he always made me miserable, even when I was the old me. He sat in his classroom wearing headphones and carrying a portable music player. Every so often he would snap his fingers or sway from side to side. Just as we were about to start studying, he screamed, "Do it to me, to me, to me-e-e-e, baby, bay-ay-ay-ay-bee-ee-ee-ee-ee."

Instead of cracking the books, everyone cracked up. Dirk wondered if Mr. Beebe should try out for *American Idol,* and that made my teammates start a whole new conversation about the show. It was probably just the thought of Mr. Beebe wailing out a tune on national TV that made my teammates crack up.

I wanted to scream at the rest of the team, *Get out your flashcards and old tests and let's start practicing already. There still might be a chance to win the Brain Bowl on Saturday!*

But instead of screaming, I forced myself to giggle along with my teammates. After all, the new Maya went along with the crowd and had a cute, fake giggle she tried to show off at any opportunity.

Bud asked me if I was okay.

I giggled even harder and threw back my shoulders. The *Teen Vogue* that Lindsey and I had read the night before said that the reverse shoulder thrust accented one's décolletage. Meaning that maybe the pose would make me look like I was bigger than a 32A on top.

"Did you hurt your back?" Bud asked.

The magazine article never mentioned that the reverse shoulder thrust could make people look injured. I told Bud I was just fine.

In the old days he would have teased me and I might have joked back, and my laughs would have been real. But that was what friends did, not possible love interests.

"Are you sure you're okay?" Bud asked.

In as bright a voice as I could muster, I repeated that I was just fine.

Lindsey popped her head in the doorway. "Hi," she said in her sweet, cheerleader voice.

Dirk waved at her wildly, and the rest of us, excluding Mr. Beebe of course, nodded or smiled at her or said hi back. I noticed that Bud's smile seemed wider than anyone's. I didn't recall him smiling so large for me. Not lately, at least.

"Maya," Lindsey said. "After you're done here, do you want to go to the Mall-O-Rama?"

A few weeks ago, I never would have thought that a social nothing like me would be invited out shopping with one of the most popular girls in school. I also never thought I'd want to turn her down. I liked Lindsey, but I had studying to do.

"I think we might be here for two or three hours getting ready for the Brain Bowl," I said. I tried to fake disappointment, putting my lips in a half-pout just like the model on this month's *Teen Vogue*.

"You look really disappointed," Rani said.

Wow! The fake worked well. Was this how Julia Roberts got her start? Maybe I should consider joining the drama club. Or I could enter one of those poker championships. My nickname could be Straight-faced Truitt.

But, really, I barely had time to practice for karate or the Brain Bowl. And those were the activities I wanted to do most—besides kissing Bud Bloom. Going shopping with Lindsey, or anyone else, would be about number fifty on my priority list.

Then Daisy suggested stopping the practice early so I could go to the mall with Lindsey.

I couldn't help thinking Daisy seemed bossy. Was that how I sounded too? Or used to sound?

"Okay with you, Maya?" Lindsey asked me.

What could I do but nod? So I did. My head felt like it had just gained twenty pounds.

"See you in sixty," Lindsey said as she left the room, swinging her hips softly as she walked.

I just knew Bud would be staring at her. But when I looked at him, it seemed he'd been staring at me. Score one for my plan.

"Since we only have an hour, let's get started," Daisy announced.

The sound of her voice must have jolted Mr. Beebe to Planet Earth. "Studying hard?" he shouted with the headphones still on.

Daisy gave him a thumbs-up.

He returned to his music player.

"Let's practice modern poetry," Daisy said.

I told myself I should be happy someone else was taking charge of the team for once. But I couldn't help thinking that I would have picked a better topic than modern poetry. After a few minutes playing Name That Poet, Daisy suggested we schedule additional practices before the County Championship.

I supposed I should have felt grateful that Daisy was filling in for me as unofficial team leader. I knew I shouldn't have felt perturbed. Feel grateful, I told myself. I unfurled my eyebrows and uncrossed my arms. Nope. It didn't work. I still felt perturbed.

Dirk, Rani, and Bud didn't seem perturbed. With their open mouths, bulgy-eyed stares at Daisy, and sudden muteness, they looked like shock victims. After a few seconds looking at the newly bossy Daisy, they all turned to look at me.

I forced myself to shrug.

Their jaws dropped about an inch in unison. Apparently, they still weren't totally used to the new Maya.

To top off my nonchalant act, I said, "Whatever, Daisy."

While I pretended I didn't care at all about practicing for the Brain Bowl, I was screaming on the inside shouting, *Of course we should practice! We will humiliate ourselves if we don't!* With my acting performances lately, I probably could have won the starring role in the school play. Actually, I bet I could have done a feature film worthy of an Oscar.

Bud asked me something. His smooth, deep voice reminded me of a vat of warm, flowing chocolate. Perhaps we could both get roles in a feature film, preferably a romance.

"Maya."

"Huh?" I asked him. (Okay, so I needed work on improvised dialogue.)

He cocked his head at me. He was luscious, even when lopsided. "I was asking you if you could you organize the additional practices."

I wanted to say, *Of course. Anything you want, sweetness.* But I had a plan to abide by. So I said, "I don't want to act like a drill sergeant. I'll just do whatever the rest of the team wants."

His mouth opened wide enough to show off his uvula.

"Besides, I'm pretty busy these days with shopping and parties and such." I tossed back my hair. Oops. It accidentally whipped Bud in the face.

That must have un-shocked him. He laughed. "Same old Maya. Always abusing me."

"I'm not the same old Maya!" I shouted. "Got that, Bud?"

He stopped laughing. He backed up.

The room went silent.

Except for Mr. Beebe, singing, "Ooh, ooh, ooh, pretty mama do me right, right, right, ri-i-i-i-ight, girl."

Everyone started laughing again, until Daisy put up her hand to keep order. "I will call or e-mail you about when we'll have our extra practices. In the meantime, we need to practice right now. Let's start with Asian dynasties," she said.

The rest of us nodded.

We focused on questions and answers for the next fifty-six minutes, until Lindsey returned to pick me up for our mall trip.

I had a much better time than I'd expected. For one thing, Lindsey was really helpful. She found me clothes that were perfect for my figure. I never realized that a simple thing like a blouse with a V-neck and horizontal stripes could make me look curvy. Or at least curvier than my usual black chopstick look. She also showed me that wearing a shirt and pants the same color could add the illusion of three extra inches in height. She didn't exactly change my Jada Pinkett Smith figure to a Halle Berry one, but she found a way to round out a few of my edges and lengthen my look.

And she was nice about it too. She wanted my opinion on clothes, and never said I looked bad, even in when I tried on a plaid outfit that made me resemble an undersized clown.

There was one problem. And it was a biggie. Buying the cute, new wardrobe Lindsey helped me pick out left me nearly broke.

The last item I bought was a pair of high-heeled shoes that hurt my feet with every aching step, but made my legs appear almost womanly. I choked up a bit as I looked through my wallet. I had a grand total of $1.47 to my name. I didn't know how I was going to tell Tiffany that I'd spent nearly everything I'd saved for my half of a karaoke machine. Though, lately, I barely had time to tell Tiffany anything at all. Or to listen to her tell me stuff, for that matter.

After we bought cookies at the food court, I was left with only fifteen cents.

Plus, I had lost valuable studying time for the Brain Bowl.

As we walked around Mall-O-Rama eating our cookies and trying to spot hot guys, Lindsey gushed about how excited was about her birthday party. "I'm so happy you're coming," she said.

"Me too." It was really hard to act enthusiastic while holding in a sigh.

Chapter 8

Though it was Friday, it was also teachers' education day, meaning there was no school. The school holiday didn't stop me from getting out of bed at dawn. I would have liked some more shut-eye, but I had ironing to do, nails to polish, an outfit to select, Brain Bowl practice to attend, and people to impress. Actually, only one person: Bud Bloom. Besides, I couldn't sleep knowing that the Brain Bowl was only one day away.

Daisy had scheduled a practice for nine a.m. at Java Jane's. I was really looking forward to it, and not just for the peppermint hot chocolate I planned to drink there. For one thing, I wouldn't have to listen to Mr. Beebe's snores or his computer game angst or his bad singing. For another, I was excited about spending all morning with a common team goal of kicking butt at tomorrow's

Brain Bowl championship game. Last but not least, I couldn't wait to see Bud Bloom.

I imagined him walking into Java Jane's and finding me at a table sipping coffee. (Bud would think it was coffee, anyway, because the new Maya was the type of woman to drink a mature quaff. Of course, I wouldn't really be drinking coffee—eww and gross. But to a bystander across the room, hot chocolate could very well be construed as coffee.) Couple the coffee facade with my new, white cotton dress and jeweled sandals, and I imagined Bud would find me worldly and sophisticated—in other words, nothing like the karate-chopping drill sergeant Maya of old.

I showed up at Java Jane's four and a half minutes early, got my drink, found a table, brought enough chairs over for the team, sat sideways with my ankles crossed to show off my legs, and waited. And waited. I took out my study materials, and waited. And waited. I tested myself with the flashcards. And waited. I knew my teammates made a habit of being late, but it was already nine twenty-one and I was the only one who had shown up.

I took out my cell phone, which was supposed to be for emergencies only, looked up Daisy's cell phone number, and called her.

"Where are you?" I asked.

"At Java Jane's, waiting for you guys."

Huh?

"Hold on," she said. "I think that's Dirk on the other line."

I tapped my finger on the table. Yikes! I just broke another nail. It was so hard to look feminine.

Daisy came back on the phone and explained everything. Apparently, she'd told people on the team to meet at Java Jane's, but hadn't told them which one. She was waiting at the Java Jane's by her house, Dirk was at the one near the library, and I was cooling my heels at the one near school.

"What about Bud and Rani?" I asked her. "I wonder which Java Jane's they went to."

"Oh no!" Daisy exclaimed. "I forgot to tell them we had practice today."

I tried to be nice about it. But I couldn't help thinking that if I had organized the practices, we'd all be in the same place, studying hard, and we wouldn't get humiliated at the County Championship.

After a few minutes of trying to hold a three-way telephone conversation, Daisy, Dirk, and I decided it was too hard and too late to get together.

Daisy said, "It sure was easier when you made the arrangements, Maya."

I told her she just needed a little more practice. To myself I added, And our team needs a lot more practice.

At least the whole day wouldn't be ruined. I still had my hairdressing appointment. I wanted to get a trim and a sophisticated updo. I arrived at Zena's a few minutes early. She had her back to me, putting the finishing touches on another girl's hair, who was about my age. The girl had long, black hair. Zena had styled it in a seventies afro with streaks of red and a colorful sash. The girl's hair looked phenomenal. But that style wasn't ladylike or feminine or delicate. It would go completely against the plan. I still wanted a sophisticated upsweep. I bit my lip. At least I'd get to hang with Zena.

When she walked over to greet me, she gave me her usual Grand Canyon smile. But as she came closer, I could see her struggle to hold it up. Then she looked me over—starting from the top of my straightened hair, down to my Sahara Sonata shadowed, Pretty in Pink rouged, Sexy Siren lipsticked face, my cotton dress, jeweled sandals, and mauve pedicured toenails. As Zena's eyes moved up and down, her smile just moved down. It changed from the Grand Canyon to an ordinary canyon, to a pothole, to a Lifesaver hole. That's when you couldn't call her expression a smile anymore. Her lips were just pursed.

Zena fingered the Z on the chain around her neck. "I see you're still bent on that crazy plan to hide your true self."

I crossed my arms. "It's not crazy."

Zena patted the end of my flip. "This style would suit a young child or maybe a monk in seclusion. But, girl, you deserve something with sparkle."

That was nice of her to say, but sparkle didn't get very far in the social strata of school. "My grandma says a true lady sparkles with good charm, not flamboyant hair," I told her.

"Your grandma also thinks the hottest singer today is Wayne Newton. Don't believe everything she says."

I crossed my arms. "I'd like a subtle yet sophisticated upsweep today. I happen to be going to a party tonight for one of the most popular girls at our school—as her personal invited guest. And that popular girl told me I look like a young Audrey Hepburn."

"Audrey Hepburn? Not only is she white, she's dead. What you want to look like an old, dead white lady for? What about your own self? What's wrong with that look?"

Everything, I thought. That look gave me nothing but trouble. "My plan is working," I told Zena.

"Then why do you seem so unhappy, baby?"

"I'm not unhap . . ." I blinked back tears. "Unhap . . ." I rubbed my eye, then worried I had raccoon-face. "I'm just fine."

Zena tried to put her arm around me.

I worried that in the comfort of Zena's big, soft embrace, I'd totally lose it. So I stepped aside, sniffed in big, and asked Zena to put my hair into an upsweep like Audrey Hepburn's.

Zena shook her big head. "Get real, Maya. An upsweep won't put any cheer into your cheeks. It wasn't even a good style forty years ago. How about we do a nice red weave and beads?'

A total violation of my plan. "No one in my school wears that style."

"All the reason for you to. Don't you want to stand out?"

I shook my head. "I want to blend in with popular girls like Lindsey Jacques. Which is what this upsweep will allow me to do."

"You get your black belt in karate, you ain't blending in. And you won't blend in winning that brain game," Zena said.

"Well, maybe I won't get my black belt, or win the Brain Bowl County Championship. Some things are more important."

Zena crossed her arms. "Girl, you are so messed up. What craziness got into that silly head of yours?"

Bud Bloom, for one thing. Though he mostly got into my heart. If I wanted to look good for him tomorrow at the Brain Bowl, I needed to get started right away. I told Zena, "I have a lot to do today. Brows to tweeze, pores to cleanse, and a party to attend. Could you just style my hair the way I want it? I mean, the way I asked?"

She closed her eyes. "That's not really how you want it."

"It is. Please, Zena."

"I did it once. I ain't doing no dumb hairstyles again."

"But I'm the customer. The customer is always right. Right?"

"You are a lot more to me than a plain old customer. Now you giving up this silliness or not?"

"Not," I said.

I could feel the tears welling up. For my own sanity, and, okay, maybe because I was a chicken, I ran out of the shop. I slowed down about a block past the beauty shop door and paced the sidewalk. I didn't need Zena hovering over me with her bright, unique caftans and her mysterious charm necklace and the advice she was always trying to give me. The new Maya didn't need advice from her or anyone else. I could do just fine by myself.

Chapter 9

I stared in the bathroom mirror as I combed out my hair. I didn't need Zena to style it, anyway. I could take care of it perfectly myself. I knew all about makeup and fashion. How hard could hairdos be? And I sure didn't need Zena giving me those dirty looks over my pretty looks. She was probably just jealous.

It was only 5:45 p.m. I still had over two hours before my mother and grandmother came home to watch Tiffany. I had plenty of time to fix myself up for Lindsey's party.

My hair looked really frizzy, bordering on ratty. I put some gel in it. Ack! That just made it look really frizzy, bordering on ratty, and greasy. I borrowed Grandma's curling iron and spent the next twenty minutes trying to get my hair in a sophisticated upsweep, but it came out all uneven. Maybe I hadn't given Zena enough credit for what she did. Making my hair look good was harder than I had thought. Making my hair look better than horrible was harder than I had thought.

I decided to get in the shower, wash my hair, and start over. I knew I should be studying—especially extinct animals and inventors, extinct or otherwise, not to mention karate moves. But Lindsey's slumber party was that evening and I didn't want my appearance to gross out the other girls.

As I soaped off in the shower, I noticed my nail polish was already chipping. I had just put that on a few nights ago. I made a mental note to touch up my nails as soon as I dried off. Speaking of mental notes, I realized I had forgotten yesterday's mental note to buy new perfume. (My bottle had spilled all over the bathroom counter.)

I'd have to use two weeks' allowance for perfume. I would never be able to buy the stuff I'd been saving for. I already owed Mom twenty dollars for Lindsey's birthday present—a pair of chandelier earrings and a CD from this indie band that was supposed to be the next big thing.

I let the shower water wash over me. I'd been so busy lately, it felt great just to stand under the faucet. At that moment, I didn't have to worry about my clothes or hair or makeup, or how others saw me.

I closed my eyes, but the peaceful feeling quickly slipped away as I thought of everything I still needed to do. It was a lot of work to be so feminine. And not much fun.

I turned off the shower and squeezed the water out of my hair. The grease was gone, but my hair still begged for attention. I didn't know what to do with it.

I dried off and sat on the bed with a towel wrapped around me. At this moment, something felt different. My shoulders weren't hunched. My breathing had slowed. I felt my lips. Holy cow, I was smiling, and it wasn't even fake. This strange feeling probably stemmed from being in the privacy of my room, and not worrying if I looked trendy or attractive enough. I was comfortable, a feeling I hadn't experienced in weeks.

I frowned. *Being comfortable won't help you win boys' hearts or popularity,* I told myself. *You need to primp for Lindsey's party.*

A hair fix was first on the agenda. I returned Grandma's curling iron and borrowed her foam curlers. She was out with her opera fan friends, but I assumed she would be thrilled to lend me her beauty tools.

Learning to use Grandma's curlers was more difficult than memorizing all the chemical elements. If I put the curlers on tightly, they hurt my scalp. If I eased up on them, they didn't hold my hair correctly. It took me approximately thirty-four minutes to get the curlers in my hair. By that time, I felt like an ogre and looked like an alien.

I was in a towel and curlers, and multitasking— reciting kings and queens of England while putting lotion on my legs and letting astringent dry on my face—when Tiffany knocked on my bedroom door.

"Is this a life-threatening emergency?" I called to her.

"Yes. Sort of," she yelled back.

"Then call nine-one-one."

She didn't laugh.

"I'm kidding," I called back.

She opened the door and furled her little eyebrows, which unfortunately reminded me again that my brows needed plucking. Ouch.

"You look strange," Tiffany said.

"Thanks. What's the emergency?"

"When are you going to help me on my emotional stuff for the election?"

"You mean promotional stuff?"

"Right, that's what I said. So, when? I keep asking you and you keep saying, 'Not today.'"

I sighed. "I've got some personal maintenance issues to take care of today. My skin, my nails, and my hair, mainly. Then I have to dress for a party." Hmm. What would one pack for a slumber party for a really popular girl? Should I take my newer nightgown, even though it's got Mickey Mouse on it, or should I bring my older one that's plain yellow, but faded?

"So if not today, when are you going to help?" Tiffany asked.

"Sorry, Tiffany. I can't today. Or tomorrow either, because that's scheduled for the Brain Bowl. If we win— which I doubt we will, given that we haven't studied enough—we'll probably go somewhere to celebrate. If we lose, I doubt I'll be in any mood to be near people. Even you, Tiffany." I smiled at her.

She didn't smile back.

I tried to think of a way to cheer her without making a time commitment to her. Aha! I snapped my fingers. I had the perfect idea. "Hey, I bet Grandma can help. She gave me great advice about improving my looks and personality."

"You think Grandma gave you great advice?" Tiffany obviously did not share my enthusiasm for the Grandma idea. "You think you've improved? Yuck!"

"You don't have to be mean about it," I said.

"I hate your new looks and your so-calling personality!"

"'So-calling'? You mean *so-called*?"

"I hate Grandma! And you too!" she shouted before racing out of my bedroom.

Wow, where did that come from? I asked myself. I guess I haven't been paying attention to her. I didn't know she was so upset.

I followed her out of the room, but she had already sprinted down the hallway. I was barely outside my bedroom doorway when she ran out the front door.

"Tiffany! Tiffany!" I called. But she was gone.

Chapter 10

I was in my towel with curlers on my head. I couldn't chase after Tiffany the way I was dressed. Or, actually, the way I was *not* dressed.

I sped back to my room and threw on the closest and easiest things I could find—my karate pants and a Mighty Minds team sweatshirt the old Maya used to wear. I didn't even bother with socks or shoes.

As I pulled the sweatshirt over my head, a few of my curlers were knocked to the carpet. I didn't have time to put them back. With my sister outside at night by herself, my appearance was the last thing I was worried about.

I ran out the front door and shouted Tiffany's name.

No answer.

"I'm sorry, Tiffany!" I yelled. "I shouldn't have been so selfish."

No answer.

I ran to the side of the house, opened the gate, and rushed into the backyard. I called her name, but still she didn't respond.

So I sped to the front yard again. The cold, damp grass felt surprisingly good under my bare soles. Being barefoot sure beat wearing the uncomfortable shoes I'd been struggling with the past few weeks. "I'll help you with your campaign, Tiffany," I shouted.

No response.

I ran up and down the block, calling Tiffany's name. What if something horrible had happened to her? She could have been kidnapped. She could have fallen and twisted her ankle and at this very instant be lying on a sidewalk somewhere. What if a vicious dog had bitten her? Or even worse, coyotes? "Tiffany! Tiffany! I'm sorry!"

I decided to call the police. I headed toward the house, calling out her name the entire way.

Before I went inside to get the phone, I made one last attempt. "Tiffany, I'm worried about you," I cried out. "I should have helped you on your campaign. I want you to win. I miss you."

"You do?" Her voice came softly, behind the large elm tree on the far right side of our front yard.

Thank goodness she was okay.

I peered at the tree. The sky was getting so dark I couldn't see much of anything. I walked toward the area where I thought I had heard her, and apologized along the way.

"Don't come closer or I'll run away for sure," she warned.

I stopped in my tracks. "Come on, Tiff. It's dangerous for you to be outside at nighttime. And Mom and Grandma will kill us if they find out."

How could I get her to return to the house? I could help her with her campaign right away, so she'd know I was sincere. But how could I do that out in the dark?

Then suddenly I remembered that strange sign on the marquee in front of the school. "Make up a slogan," it had said. "If you come back, I'll try to think of some campaign slogans for you, okay?" I shouted.

No answer.

"How's this: Here's an epiphany. Vote for Tiffany."

"What's a piphany?" She stepped forward, to a spot in front of the tree.

"It's a realization about something important," I said. "Epiphany. Like I just realized how much I'd rather spend my time hanging with you than doing my nails and stuff."

"I don't think the other kids in my class will know what that piphany thing is."

"Come into the house and we can think of something else together," I suggested.

Silence.

I thought hard. "How about, Don't be hesitant. Vote Tiffany for President?"

"Hesident is still too hard of a word." She crossed her arms. "Your slogans stink, Maya. You don't even care if I win the election. If you were making up a slogan about yourself or that Bud guy, you'd try a lot harder."

I shook my head. "How could you say that to me, Tiff?"

"Because the last few weeks you've been all into yourself. That's how."

"I haven't been into myself. Not exactly. I've been into makeup and perfume and clothes."

It hit me. Tiffany was right. This wasn't being myself at all. I'd been into covering myself up, trying to create a fake version of myself, as if my real self weren't good enough.

"Well, you haven't been into me," Tiffany said.

"I haven't been into you, or karate, or preparing for the Brain Bowl. I've been neglecting everything I love most. What an idiot I've been. My slogan should be: Maya Truitt really blew it. The fact is, Tiff, I thought I should be a different type of person. But, to say it in a slogan, I have no passion for high fashion. And, Makeup makes me break up. Now I realize I should accept myself for who I am. And I see what a mistake it was to ignore you, Tiff. So I'm campaigning right now, as hard as I can, to get you back. How's this for my slogan: I really miss my little sis?"

Tiffany laughed. "Do you really?" Her little, shadowy figure finally started walking toward me.

Phew.

But what was that? Someone, a very tall person, was coming up the sidewalk, our way. How long had he been here? What was he doing there?

I screamed. "Tiffany, watch out!"

"Watch out for what?" she said.

The large figure kept clumping toward us. Tiffany was walking right in his path.

I wished I hadn't slacked off on my karate practice lately. I was going to need all my training. At least I had on my karate pants. I tried to think quickly about the best move against this giant man. Sensei George said physical strength was not as important as mental cunning. I'd have to take this brute down by surprise.

Of course! I'd use a jumping scissors takedown. I raced toward him on my tiptoes to surprise him. As soon as I got close enough, I jumped and came down hard, clamping my right leg behind his knees and my left leg on his chest. Just as I'd practiced, the jumping scissors made him fall on his back. I sat behind him with my legs grasping him tight. As I trapped him, I shouted, "Don't make a move, jerkface!"

Chapter 11

"The 'jerkface' you just attacked is me," Bud Bloom said.

Oh no! I'd done it again. Poor Bud! Poor me!

"Uh, Maya, could you let go, please?" he said.

"What's going on?" my sister asked.

"I screwed up, that's what's going on," I said. "I just tried to beat up Bud Bloom. Again."

I released my legs and tried to stand up and walk away. But I fell over and ended up splayed on the grass.

Bud managed to sit up. Meanwhile, Tiffany hurried over to me. Each of them grabbed one of my hands and helped me to my feet. I felt mega-humiliated. I also couldn't help noticing how good my hand felt in his. But the mortification was overwhelming, and I dropped my hand.

"I am so, so sorry," I told Bud. "And I already apologized to you, Tiff."

"I heard your apology. 'Maya Truitt really blew it.' " He laughed. "You've got talent."

I moaned. "You heard everything? All those stupid slogans?"

"They weren't *all* stupid," Tiffany said in my defense. "Only most of them."

"At least you sounded like the old Maya, the Maya I know and lo—er, like," Bud said. "You sounded like you again, instead of some phony fashionista."

"Phony fashionista?" That didn't sound like a good thing. My plan had been to make Bud like the new me. But Bud seemed as if he loathed the new me.

"I just . . ." He cleared his throat. "You've been acting a tad, well, weird the last few weeks."

Weird? That didn't sound like a good thing either. Speaking of weird, I felt my hair. Ack! It still had curlers in it. But there was a big section on the right where the curlers must have fallen off, probably during my attack on Bud. Grandma was not going to be amused to find grass stains on her curlers.

I bet my crazy getup tonight amused Bud. Sigh. Even the old Maya wouldn't want to be seen in a hairstyle-in-progress, old sweatshirt, and karate pants.

"Don't tell anyone how awful I look now," I told him. "Or I'll show you my killer karate Shuto strike."

He laughed. "I think you look kind of cute."

Did Bud Bloom just call me kind of cute?

"But please don't hurt me. I don't think I can take any more." He crossed his arms over his chest as a mock defense. Or possibly a real defense.

"Why are you here, anyway?" I asked him.

"You know, that's not the most friendly thing anyone's ever said to me."

"You want friendly?" I gave him a friendly punch on the shoulder. Just like old times. Ooh, my hand tingled where I had touched his broad, masculine shoulder.

"I came by to tell you how much I appreciate what you've done for the team, Maya. Though I used to complain about you nagging—"

"Nagging?"

"Let me rephrase that. Gentle reminding. Anyway, we need your encouragement. Otherwise, we'd end up wasting time, getting the practice locations mixed up, and slacking off way too much."

I was glad it was dark, because otherwise he'd be sure to see my ear-to-ear grin.

"I behaved like a doofus. I want to make it up to you. Let me take you out for ice cream."

My grin got so wide it hurt my face. But I didn't mind.

"But not until the County Championship is over," Bud added. "We need to devote our free time to studying for it."

"You've got yourself a deal," I said.

We shook on it. He had the softest, warmest hand in the universe. Not that I'd felt every hand in the universe, but I couldn't imagine anything softer or warmer. I got a tad teary when we let our hands go.

I tried to get my mind off how crazy he made me. I didn't want to start acting foolish. More foolish, anyway, than shouting silly slogans outside in curlers and old clothes and performing a jumping scissors takedown on the love of my life. I told myself to think about something else besides Bud Bloom. "Um, speaking of ice cream," I said, "Did you know that Thomas Jefferson was one of the first people to introduce ice cream in America?"

"I didn't know that," Bud said. "But I'm glad you told me."

"Thomas Jetson is the guy who invented the telephone, right?" Tiffany asked.

"It's Jefferson, not Jetson," I said. "He didn't invent the telephone, but he did a lot of other stuff, like designed this amazing house in Virginia called Monticello. And of course he was our third president. Tiff, did you know he died—"

"The same day as John Adams," Bud said. "This stuff is so fascinating."

"I know," I said. "July Fourth—"

"1826," Bud and I said together.

I always knew he was my soul mate.

"How about getting in a little Brain Bowl practice right now?" Bud asked.

A study session with Bud Bloom? Just the two of us sharing flashcards? I was totally tempted. But I couldn't break my promise to Lindsey. "I'd love to practice with you, Bud. But I'm supposed to go to Lindsey Jacques's slumber party tonight. And also I need to help my sister."

"Yeah, Bud," Tiffany said. "Wait your turn."

"As you heard, I told my sister I'd help her with her campaign. I'm going to start tonight. And tomorrow, Tiffany and I are going to play Frisbee. There's this new throw I'm dying to try."

Bud nodded. "Hey, speaking of new throws. When you have more time, can you show me that karate throw you used on me? I might have to enroll in your studio, just for my own defense."

"You're kidding, right?"

"Actually, no. If I did karate, I might be the only Jewish, Brain Bowl expert, karate student for miles around. That would be so cool."

"Cool? You don't mind being different?" I couldn't help asking.

"That's what makes people so attractive, don't you think?"

Didn't I think? No, I couldn't think of anything beyond that Bud Bloom was standing in my very own front yard, talking about what made people attractive. I closed my eyes so he wouldn't distract me so much. Somewhere in the fuzzy recesses of my tired brain, I think he was saying that uniqueness was a plus. I could definitely go with that.

"I'd better let you do all that stuff you have planned for tonight. You're not staying over at Lindsey's, are you?"

"I told her I would."

He got on one knee. Bud Bloom, in all his total cuteness and niceness and smartness, was perched on his knee four inches beside me. Maybe five inches. But, still, really close.

I had the feeling—a quite frightening feeling, to be honest—that he was going to propose.

Instead, he clasped his hands together and begged. "Please don't go there. Slumber parties are notorious for girls staying up all hours into the morning. And then you'll be too tired for the County Championship game tomorrow. We can't have that happen to the most valuable member of the team. We all need you. I need you."

If someone had told me Bud Bloom would be on his knees in front of my house declaring that he needed me, I never, ever would have believed it. I closed my eyes again to savor the moment.

"What does *torious* mean?" Tiffany asked, putting a major damper on the moment.

"Torious? Oh, *notorious*. Famous in a negative way," Bud said from his kneeling position.

What a total genius. And a babe. And a guy who wasn't afraid to admit he needed me.

Bud broke into my reverie. "My knees are killing me. Please say you won't stay up too late tonight. And say it soon. I'd hate to be down here begging all night."

I couldn't help laughing. "Maybe I can just stay for a few hours, and then crash in my own bed. If you promise to study really hard tonight, I'll call Lindsey and tell her I need to leave early."

Bud got to his feet. "The drill sergeant's back." He seemed quite happy about that.

So was I.

I actually made two calls. I took the phone into my bedroom, closed the door, took a deep breath, and punched in Lindsey's number. I told her that I was sorry, but I had to leave the party by 10:30.

"I totally understand," she said.

I fell back on my bed. "You do?"

"Yes. I want you to be wide awake tomorrow so you can, like, make the school proud."

Lindsey wanted me to make the school proud. What a relief. I hadn't realized winning the Brain Bowl would make anyone at school proud, except me and the other members of the nerd contingent. That made me happy, but not completely. No one would be proud of my appearance. Especially not Lindsey Jacques, who always looked perfect.

I took another deep breath before telling her my additional news. "I was supposed to get my hair done today, but I stupidly left the beauty shop before my appointment."

"Stupidly?" she said. "You're not stupid. I'm sure there was a good reason."

"There wasn't, actually. It was stupid. Even Brain Bowl members can act like idiots sometimes." At that moment, I felt like I could win a County Brainless Bowl championship. "What I'm trying to say, Lindsey, is that my hair looks atrocious. Plus, the polish on my fingernails is as chipped as a Tollhouse cookie. If I took the time to fix my hair and nails before your party tonight, I wouldn't have a chance to cram for the Brain Bowl tomorrow or keep a promise to my little sister. I'm really sorry."

"I'm hurt," Lindsey said.

Just as I suspected. "You think I should spend more time primping for your big birthday bash, right? I know it's really important to you, and I'm going to look like a slob."

"That's not it at all. I'm hurt because you think I care so much about minor things like your hair and your nails."

"You don't?"

"Geez, Maya, how shallow do you think I am? I like you for you. For your personality and your accomplishments. And also because you treat me so nicely. You're one of the few people who seem to enjoy me for who I am, not just because you think I'm pretty or popular."

I had totally underestimated Lindsey Jacques. I had been so worried about the assumptions people might make about me that I had made silly assumptions about Lindsey. Yep, I deserved the Brainless Bowl title. Especially because Lindsey was a fantastic friend. Hearing her say she liked me for my accomplishments and personality made me so happy. Not quite as happy as I felt when Bud Bloom held my hand. Nothing could compete with Bud's magnificent palm.

I apologized again before hanging up. Since it was Lindsey's birthday, and because I had to save some of my communication skills for my next call, I put off telling her that I planned to return the clothes I had bought with her at the mall. Except the way cute blouse with the horizontal stripes, and the funky mauve boots. I did like dressing up, sometimes.

The next call I had to make was harder, but even more necessary.

As soon as Zena said hello, I told her I was sorry.

She didn't respond. I pictured her sitting in the big purple chair at the front of the shop, one hand swinging the Z charm hanging from her neck.

Finally, she said, "You come to your senses, girl? 'Cause I was just about to come by and knock some into you, brown belt or not."

"I came to my senses, Zena. I should have come to them a lot earlier."

She sniffled. Just a little, but I heard it. She wasn't as tough as she liked to let on.

"It was rude of me to walk out on you," I said. "And extremely stupid. Do you know how bad my hair looks? I never realized what a hard job you have."

She laughed. "You have that tendency toward nasty old frizz if you don't contain it good."

"Now you tell me," I said. "I need to reschedule, and soon."

"But not before that Brain Bowl of yours. You got to do good. I sure am counting on that. Don't waste that big old brain of yours."

"I'll try not to. I learned my lesson. Will you think of me tomorrow, while I'm sweating out the answers?"

"My heart will be at that contest, you know that."

"And *my* heart's feeling a lot better now. Thanks."

I set down the phone and walked toward Tiffany's room, calling out campaign slogans along the way. "Make a diff. Vote for Tiff." Or how about, "Tiffany Truitt can really do it?" Or, "Only a stiff wouldn't vote for Tiff?"

It was late, my hair was a mess, I'd attacked Bud again, he'd seen me wearing curlers and a weird outfit, and he'd heard me shouting out dumb slogans about myself.

And I felt great.

Chapter 12

I spent twenty-two minutes helping Tiffany with her campaign, and twenty-two minutes after that studying the Olympics, contemporary wars, and Chinese dynasties. Adapting my newfound slogan-composing skills, I created a birthday poem for Lindsey. "Happy Birthday to Lindsey Jacques, a pretty girl who really rocks. You're a good friend who's always well dressed. You're totally nice and deserve the best." I slipped in the poem along with an invitation to hang at my house with the earrings and CD I'd bought for her.

That night I had focused on what really mattered. Consequently, I used very little of my time on my appearance, and it showed. I hadn't applied makeup or even a spritz of perfume. The blouse I wore could have used a good ironing, but I hadn't had time. I arrived at

Lindsey's slumber party with hair that looked like the grand finale of a fireworks show and nail polish so old and spotty my fingertips looked like modern art.

Even though I'd given up on my plan to look ladylike all the time, I knew my appearance still mattered—a little to me and a lot to other people. I hoped Lindsey and her friends at the party wouldn't be appalled by my looks. I made myself shrug before I knocked on Lindsey's door.

Her parents answered, holding hands. Lindsey obviously had gotten her mom's big, sky blue eyes and heart-shaped face and her dad's thick blond hair. As for Lindsey's big, toothy smile, which seemed to be a permanent part of her, it was hard to tell because both her parents beamed at me with similar big, toothy smiles.

"Welcome, dear," Lindsey's mom said. She had what appeared to be a large burn scar covering the right side of her nose and her right cheek.

"Hi." I smiled back at her. "I'm Maya Truitt."

As Ms. Jacques ushered me into the house, she said, "So you're the Brain Bowl girl. Lindsey goes on and on about how smart you are." She said it like it was a great thing.

My smile grew even larger.

"Mom, don't embarrass me," Lindsey protested, as she walked toward us. She looked beautiful as usual.

Her white miniskirt showed off her long legs and her bright pink lipstick highlighted her sweet face.

"I'm the embarrassed one." I pointed to my sorry-looking hair. "I don't usually look like this."

"You have more important things to worry about, like the County Championship game tomorrow," Lindsey said.

More important? Lindsey Jacques believed preparing for the Brain Bowl was more important than looking good? Wow. Before, I had assumed she would say that nothing was more important than looking good.

"We'll be upstairs playing chess," Mr. Jacques said. "We've got a lot of practicing to do. The last time one of us beat Lindsey was in 2005."

"You—" I could barely get the words out. "Lindsey, you play chess?"

"Keep that quiet, okay?" Her cheeks were bright pink and it wasn't just from her makeup.

"That's a good thing," I told her. "You should be proud."

She shrugged. "Thanks."

"Dance contest!" someone yelled from the back of the house. "Come on, everyone!"

"Awesome!" Lindsey shouted. "Let's go, Maya."

I didn't win the dance contest. I didn't even come close. But I did have a lot of fun. Then Juanita Perez showed off some cheerleading moves and Lara Taylor tried to teach us pirouettes. I knew Juanita was a cheerleader, but I never realized before that Lara was so into ballet. I demonstrated a front-ball karate kick. The girls seemed impressed. For a minute, anyway.

Lindsey said, "Speaking of kicks, has anyone seen our hot new soccer goalie?" That got us all talking about the cutest guys in school. I didn't mention Bud Bloom, but I definitely was thinking of him.

The girls were better dressed and coiffed than me. And that came in handy. What could be more useful than five other girls anxious to style me? Well, Zena could be more useful, but this was the next best thing to her. The girls managed to get my hair looking almost normal, thanks to a curling iron, a few handfuls of gel, and a lot of effort. Then we all did one another's nails. Lindsey even spelled out "I love facts" across my fingernails. The girls were amazed when I told them that nail polish was first used in China over five thousand years ago.

After that, someone started a Truth or Dare game. I was so worried one of the girls would ask if I had a crush on anyone. I would have to do a dare rather than admit I liked Bud. And the dares were not easy. Mandy Hess had to perform a chicken dance on the front porch, and Juanita Perez had to drink a mixture of 7-Up, Diet Pepsi, and water.

Then Juanita asked Lindsey to name the most embarrassing TV show she watches.

Lindsey started giggling. "This is so dumb. It's, like, an eighties show I've been watching since I was a kid. It's totally embarrassing that I still like it. I can't say."

Juanita threatened her with a dare.

Finally, Lindsey, still laughing, said, "I admit I'm semi-addicted to *Full House.*"

Wow! I wanted to shout "Me too!" and hug her. I didn't, actually, because it was silly to embarrass myself in front of everyone. But I planned to tell Lindsey later.

It was already 10:29 before anyone asked me a question.

"Tell the truth," Lindsey said. "Do you really like wearing the dresses and high heels I've seen you in the last few weeks?"

I was clearing my throat and looking at the ground when Ms. Jacques interrupted our game to tell me that my mom was waiting for me at the front door.

Phew! Good timing. Everyone wished me luck and I was completely out of there.

In the car, Mom had great news. The case she'd been working so hard on had settled out of court. She would have a lot more time for us now. She was even planning to take a few days off during the coming week. She offered to take me to the mall.

I held back on making choking sounds. I told her, "I'm happy you'll have more time at home, Mom. And no offense, but I don't want to look at, or even think about, new clothes for a long time." I had a better idea. "How about we go bowling one night? The whole family could come. You know how Tiffany loves bowling especially."

"But your grandmother will complain again. She broke a nail last time and vowed to never pick up a bowling ball again."

I frowned. "Her loss, I guess. She can watch us while we all have fun."

Mom asked what I'd done today while she'd been at the office negotiating the settlement.

I thought back to the Java Jane's mix-up this morning, walking out on Zena in the afternoon, my struggles to style my hair, the tiff with Tiffany, my assault on Bud, our moonlit talk afterward, and the non-slumber part of Lindsey's slumber party. I was too exhausted to even begin telling Mom all that had happened. I said, "Just a normal day for me, Mom."

I don't know if she believed me, because I fell asleep in the car.

Chapter 13

$\boldsymbol{1}$ woke up at five o'clock in the morning, completely panicked. I felt like a weakling in so many subjects: anatomy, English poets, ancient Greece, composers, and just about everything else in the universe that could exist, whether in the past or the possible future. I was so nervous about the Brain Bowl that there was no way I could get back to sleep.

I figured I might as well study. I didn't have to be in the auditorium until eleven o'clock. I needed only twenty-six minutes to shower, eat, and throw on some clothes, and twelve minutes to get there. So I had approximately five hours and twenty-two minutes to cram my head full of facts about America, the world, and the universe, and philosophies and literature about America, the world, and the universe. A breeze, I tried to reassure myself as I jumped out of bed and ran toward my study guides.

I barely looked up from my materials until eight thirty-two, when a knock on my bedroom door interrupted me.

"I'm studying!" I called out.

"You need nourishment," Grandma said.

She was always after me about something. Wait until she found out I was ditching the dresses and makeup. It would probably be the worst day of her life.

She knocked again.

I shook my head, walked over to the door, and let her in.

She was carrying a tray with one of her homemade extra-blueberry, extra-banana muffins, a mound of hot scrambled eggs, and a glass of fresh-squeezed grapefruit juice. "If your mom complains about eating in your bedroom, tell her Grandma said it was okay."

"Oh, wow."

"You may not realize it, Maya, but I'm rooting for you to beat the pants off the other team." She lifted her fist in the air. "Go out and kick some booty."

"Grandma!"

She cleared her throat. "I mean to say, I wish you well. No matter what you look like on the outside—

though I prefer a fresh coat of lipstick, a feminine dress, and ladylike posture—no matter what, I am proud of who you are."

I smiled at her.

"You do realize that your brows need a good tweezing, don't you, dear?" Grandma said.

My smile drooped a little. "Thank you."

Grandma gave me a quick hug, commented on my morning breath, and headed out of my bedroom, shouting as she left, "Take no prisoners!"

I wolfed down my delicious breakfast, studied for two more hours, and hightailed it to the Brain Bowl tournament.

By the time I got to the auditorium, my nerves were relatively calm. At least calm related to Rani's nerves, anyway. She stood with me onstage, peeking out behind the closed curtain every so often, and chattering as if a crazed woodpecker had flown into her mouth.

"We'll breeze right through this," I tried to assure her.

"I'm telling you, Maya, I have never been so nervous in my life. Except for when I thought I saw Justin Timberlake in the mall. But that turned out to be someone else, anyway. And, anyway, he likes blondes."

"Cameron Diaz," I couldn't help adding. "She rose to fame in the movie *The Mask* with—"

Rani interrupted me, "Jim Carrey, of course. Ooh, I hope they test us on pop culture. You know who else was in *Charlie's Angels* besides Cameron Diaz, right? Do you think they could ask what band Justin Timberlake played in? Oh my gosh, I'm going to blow the Brain Bowl in front of all these people."

She needed a chill pill. An extra-strength one. Immediately.

"I was just out there in the audience a few minutes ago," I told Rani. "It's not that crowded. See?"

I peered out the curtain. Yikes! There were a lot more people now. It suddenly felt like the woodpecker had gotten into my stomach.

I looked at my family for support. Mom sat in the fourth row, with Grandma and Tiffany next to her. Next to Tiffany was Lindsey Jacques. I really appreciated her coming. She had to be totally exhausted after the slumber party. As if to prove my point, she let out a giant yawn. Mr. Beebe, next to her, yawned too. At least he was awake for once. I squinted my eyes. Good. He hadn't brought in any headphones. Behind him was Mrs. Bennett, our old faculty advisor. In her arms was a blue blanket that presumably contained her new baby boy.

I nudged Rani and pointed to Mrs. Bennett. "Look who's here with her baby. How sweet is that?"

"Sweet? You mean scary." Rani clutched my arm. "Oh, gawd. I'm going to humiliate myself in front of all these people, including Mrs. Bennett. She is going to be so disappointed in me. I'll probably bring her to tears, and she'll never come back to advise our team, and we'll be stuck with Mr. Beebe as our advisor forever. Oh, I just don't think I can do this, Maya."

Rani had really lost it. I pulled her back behind the curtain. It was time for me to take charge again. "We need you on this team," I told Rani. "You're our literature expert. No one knows poets, novelists, or philosophers like you do."

"But I don't know anything now. I'm so nervous, I bet I couldn't even tell you that Mark Twain's real name is Samuel Clemens."

"You just did."

"Oh. Well, that was just a lucky guess. And I don't even know *Tom Sawyer* was published in 1876 and *Huckleberry Finn* came out in 1884. Oops, I guess I do know that. But I probably don't know a lot of other stuff and I'm going to choke onstage with gazillions of people watching me, and—"

"Try this," I interrupted. "Repeat the following, ten times. Make that twenty times. Say, My name is Rani and I'm really brawny."

"What?"

"Please, Rani, just try it."

She shrugged and then followed my instructions. After about the eighth repetition of "My name is Rani and I'm really brawny," she was smiling. By the twelfth time, she was giggling. At approximately number eighteen, she was laughing so hard she could barely get the slogan out.

I patted her shoulder. "You're going to do great."

She giggled a little more before thanking me. "That's just what I needed, Maya. I appreciate you stepping in like that."

We were still giggly when Bud, Dirk, and Daisy joined us onstage. Bud was wearing a sports jacket and Dockers. Even though the jacket sleeves barely went to his wrists, I couldn't help thinking ooh la la.

Daisy called everyone into a huddle. "Let's get serious about winning," she said. "I wish we had been more studious, like Maya."

"It's good to be well-prepared, and I think we are," I said. "But I want you all to know even if we fail miserably, we've still succeeded. I've loved being on this team and learning and getting to know you all." I couldn't help glancing at Bud and thinking, especially you.

"Hear, hear," Bud said. "Win or lose, we have a fantastic team."

"Group hug," Daisy called out.

I wished I had been standing next to Bud, instead of between Daisy and Rani. But the hug still warmed my heart. When the curtain opened, we were all still hugging.

We shook hands with the other team, and then were introduced individually. I almost fainted when Bud was introduced. It turns out *Bud* is just a nickname. His real name is Cornelius.

Rani started giggling again. Daisy whispered, "Poor thing. No wonder he goes by a nickname." Bud's face turned hot pink.

My heart beat faster. I thought Cornelius was the most brilliant, manly, original name I had ever heard.

The first question was about *Hamlet*. Rani beat everyone to the buzzer and scored us the first point.

The next question was about also-rans for president. That was on our study agenda the day we all met at different Java Jane's and canceled practice. The Saint Mary Smarties got a point for that.

The next question was a football question. Sports was our weak point, except for martial arts, of course, though some have debated whether it's a sport; ice skating, which Daisy enjoys; surfing (Dirk, totally); and badminton, Bud's sport, which unfortunately had never been a topic in the seventy-two-year history of the Brain Bowl. The Smarties answered the football question correctly (Los Angeles Rams) and pulled ahead.

But we soon evened the score with our knowledge of biology, Greek myths, and the Oscars. After Dirk answered the question about Katherine Hepburn correctly, he winked at me. I had quizzed him on it a few weeks ago.

We were playing strongly, but the Smarties weren't slouches either. It was anyone's game. By intermission, when we were given five minutes to stretch our legs and try to relax our minds, the Smarties were ahead by two points.

I looked at the audience for support. Mrs. Bennett was gazing down at her baby and stroking his thick, black hair. He was quite adorable, and I could almost see why she hadn't been there for us the past few months.

Two rows behind her sat Zena, holding her hand over her chest. I imagined she was fingering her special necklace. She wore her hair dyed purple, cornrowed, and strung with red beads. She looked fantastic. When I caught Zena's eye and smiled, she sprang from her seat, shouting, "You go, girl. It's all you, baby!"

The 4.5 zillion people in the audience stared at her, the vast majority likely frowning. Probably the only person who didn't look at Zena was Mr. Beebe. He had his eyes closed and his head on a scowling man seated next to him. He appeared to be snoring.

Zena seemed to enjoy the audience's attention. She smiled brightly and waved at me like she was signaling a rescue plane.

Beside me, Rani whispered, "You must be so embarrassed."

"Not at all," I said, before blowing Zena a kiss.

Then Mom—my very own mother who at the moment was wearing her usual weekend attire of a sensible polo shirt and khakis and beige flats—put her fingers in her mouth and blew the loudest wolf whistle I had ever heard in my life and probably ever would hear.

Grandma reached over in an attempt to remove Mom's hand from her mouth, but Mom wouldn't let her.

Watching the people who loved me increased my confidence by approximately a factor of 12.3. I knew whether we won or lost the championship, my family and friends were proud of me, and I had spent an enjoyable year learning and hanging with my teammates.

And I came to that conclusion without even thinking of Bud.

But I still really wanted to win. I made up another slogan to try to fire up my teammates. I quietly chanted, "We've studied a lot. We're in the know. Show 'em what we've got. Let's go, go, go."

After a few repetitions, my whole team was chanting this, with broad smiles on our faces. When the break ended, we were still grinning.

Dirk correctly answered the first question about Einstein's last theorem.

Next, Bud solved an algebra problem to tie up the score.

Then I got a wonderful gift. The question was, "What is a name for a karate studio?" Easy as pie. A dojo, of course. Somebody up there liked me.

But as soon as we pulled ahead, the Smarties tied it up with their knowledge of the Suez Canal.

The second half of the game proved as close as the first half, with our team pulling ahead, then the Smarties gaining on us, then us catching up, et cetera.

We had a minute left in the competition when the next category was announced: television trivia.

Groan. I hardly ever watched TV. Last week I'd seen a fascinating documentary on the lifecycle of the ringworm, and three days ago I had caught the first eight minutes of the news. But other than that, I hadn't watched a thing.

The announcer read the question. "Name the three main male characters on the show *Full House*."

Bingo! I banged on my buzzer. "Danny, Jessie, and Joey."

"Correct, to tie up the game."

My teammates stared at me open-mouthed.

I beamed.

I knew Lindsey must have been beaming back at me in the audience. That is, if she hadn't fallen asleep.

"Last question," the announcer said, and I readied my hand over the buzzer. "Which U.S. president introduced ice cream to Americans?"

Bud slammed his hand over his buzzer and jumped out of his chair. "Thomas Jefferson," he said. He added, "Our third president." Then he said, "A wonderful girl told me about that. She's—"

"Correct," the announcer said. "And the Mighty Minds win the game!"

Holy mackerel, we won! We won!

After shaking hands with the Smarties, my teammates and I jumped up and down and hugged one another. We won, we won, we won! Somehow, I ended up next to Bud in the hug. (Okay, it was due to my clever manipulation. A big brain can really help a gal when it comes to positioning oneself to hug one's crush.) And that was probably the smartest thing I ever did.

Chapter 14

It was the best day of my life. Having our team win was made even better by the humongous amount of people rooting for us. We didn't have a chance to stay in our group hug very long because a mass of fans were clamoring onstage.

As our team was being pulled apart by circling well-wishers, Bud Bloom managed to thank me for urging us to study, and to remind me that we were still on for ice cream. Then he was quickly grabbed in a parental bear hug. His dad has an even bigger afro than Bud's, only his is white. His mom is a plus-plus-plus-sized woman who wore pink overalls and a huge grin.

Mr. Beebe came onstage and took a bow, and then another, and another. I wished someone would take him off with a giant wooden hook.

By his fourth bow, I couldn't stand it anymore. I made up another slogan and started chanting it quietly, "Mr. Beebe, please, we beg you to leave." Soon, everyone on my team was whispering the slogan with me, and with a scowl Mr. Beebe scurried off the stage. I doubted anyone was sorry to see him go.

Then our team shouted for Mrs. Bennett to come up. She did, with her adorable baby, and we all hugged her. Nova Darling even walked onstage with her guitar and serenaded the baby with a lullaby. They were a wonderful few moments.

Except it lasted just a few moments. The baby let out a loud and extremely stinky poop, and Mrs. Bennett rushed off to change him.

Meanwhile, Carmen Bernstein was scribbling notes on a large tablet next to me. She said, "This will make a great article for the school paper. Page one, baby!"

For a second I worried about the publicity. Being on page one of the newspaper meant I wouldn't be able to hide my nerdiness from anyone at school. It struck me, though, that probably most people had a nerdy side, and so I shouldn't feel so embarrassed. In fact, I might be in the minority for finding the Brain Bowl to be a nerdy activity. Nova Darling didn't seem embarrassed to be strumming her guitar and singing a lullaby in front of everyone. And Carmen Bernstein seemed really proud of being on the school newspaper. So what if I was the only African-American, karate-loving, slogan-creating trivia expert for miles around? Most other kids had unique characteristics and interests too.

Lindsey stumbled up the stage stairs to congratulate me. Even when she was exhausted, she still looked gorgeous. The red in her eyes actually complimented her red lips.

"How late did you stay up this morning?" I asked.

She yawned. "Until four a.m. I'm wiped. Totally wiped."

"I can tell. I really appreciate you coming out today."

"I couldn't miss it. What do you mean 'I can tell?' Do I look that bad?"

"Lindsey, you could never look bad," I said.

"I was too tired to put on makeup or do my hair. I don't usually go out like this."

Her face was paler than usual, and her hair lay flat. But Lindsey was beautiful whether she wore makeup and styled hair or went for the natural look.

"You always look gorgeous," I told her.

She smiled. "Thanks. And you showed off that awesome brainpower of yours. Maya, would you mind if I told you something in private? It should just take a minute or two."

"No problem," I said.

But I was worried. I figured Lindsey was going to tell me I had something on my teeth. That would be so like me to embarrass myself in front of my family and friends, not to mention Bud and half the school.

We walked to the apron upstage.

"I have a secret to tell you," Lindsey said.

I ran my tongue along the front of my teeth. I didn't feel anything, but that didn't mean something ugly wasn't brewing in there. Or maybe I had a stain on my shirt that I hadn't noticed. Or dandruff.

"What is it?" I practically shouted from my nerves.

"Do you think I have any kind of chance of being on the team next year? It seems, like, really fun, and it would be so cool to hang with you at practices and stuff."

Cool? Did Lindsey Jacques just say it would be cool to hang with me? And not just *cool*, but *so cool*. Wow. That was just, well, cool. So cool.

Lindsey shrugged her dainty shoulders. Even her shoulders were pretty.

"By the shocked expression on your face, Maya, I can tell you think it's a bad idea. I don't have a chance, right?"

I shook my head. "It's not that at all. Sorry. I just didn't know you were interested in being in the Brain Bowl. I'd love it if you were on my team."

And I wasn't just saying that. I liked being around Lindsey, and it had nothing to do with her looks or popularity. It did at first, but I had realized that she was a fun girl and super nice.

"You have a chance," I told her. "Especially if you let me coach you. Since Mr. Beebe took over, I've had to be the de facto coach anyway. And I'm pretty darn good at it, if I do say so myself."

"I bet you are. That would be awesome."

"Here." I took my flashcards out of my purse. "Take these. Why don't you look at them for, like, a half hour every day? Then you can come over next weekend and I'll quiz you."

"Cool."

Cool. Another *cool* from Lindsey. Lindsey Jacques just said it was cool to practice for the Brain Bowl.

Well, it is, I reminded myself. "After we study, we could watch TV together. I have a bunch of stuff recorded that I know we'll both enjoy."

"*Full House?*"

I giggled.

"Ooh, that Jessie's so cute."

"I like Danny the best," I said.

"Danny? But he's so geeky."

"I'm kind of attracted to geeky guys."

"Like Bud Bloom?"

I giggled again. "How did you know?"

"Just by little hints you've dropped, such as every time you're within fifty feet of him, your eyes bug out like they're going to explode."

Yikes. I didn't know it was so obvious.

"Don't worry, I won't tell anyone," Lindsey said. Then she confessed she had a crush on Dirk.

My teammate Dirk? Shocker. He was a nice guy and everything, but not really my idea of crush material. Oh, wait. That explained why Lindsey kept dropping by practice—to flirt with Dirk, not with Bud.

Lindsey yawned, said she needed a nap, congratulated me again, and said good-bye.

As I watched her leave, I thought of everyone who had cheered me on and our team victory and Bud asking me out for ice cream afterward. I said to myself, This is the best day of my life.

I clutched my trophy, a replication of Rodin's *Thinker*

sculpture, which I couldn't wait to bring home. Then I noticed a thin silver bracelet around the Thinker's neck. Funny, I didn't remember it there when the announcer handed me the trophy.

I took the bracelet off the Thinker and stared at it in my palm. Dangling from the bracelet was a little charm, a T-shirt with the slogan "Smarts Rule." I had proven myself smart, not just today when our team won the tournament. I was smart enough to understand what was really important to me: karate and Tiffany and the Brain Bowl and, most of all, being myself.

I said a new slogan in my head. Maya Truitt: Smart enough to do it. Then I tried out another slogan. Black, smart, and strong. I can't go wrong.

I tried to close the bracelet around my wrist, but it was hard to fasten with one hand.

"Need help?" Zena stood next to me, carrying a large, black leather-bound notebook.

I hadn't realized she was even onstage.

"That charm suits you perfectly." She clasped the bracelet around my wrist.

"Thank you," I said. "Now we both have charms."

Zelda fingered the *Z* around her neck. "Sure enough, Maya. And we earned those."

"Where did you get your charm, anyway?"

She winked at me before looking away.

"You didn't have anything to do with my new charm, did you?"

"You earned it all by yourself, honey. You yourself had everything to do with it." She handed me the notebook.

"What's this?"

"It belongs to you."

It smelled like new leather. I rifled through it. The pages were crisp and blank, filled with possibilities.

"It's really nice, but it's not mine. Where did you find that?" I asked Zena.

There was no answer. I looked up. Zena had left the stage and was making her way out of the auditorium.

I called her name. She didn't even slow down, though she did smile at me and wave.

I flipped through the thick, blank pages. They seemed so inviting. I suddenly felt compelled to write in the notebook, to record the story about how I earned my charm. I thought I should begin it with the day I had put Bud in a hammerlock, been teased about being a drill sergeant, and broken the glass on Mom's diploma. I had thought that day was terrible, but actually it may have been the best of my life. Because it was then that I began my discovery that being an

African-American, fact-loving, slogan-making karate expert was totally cool.

I took out a pen from my purse and murmured, "Black, smart, and strong. I can't go wrong."

It's truth or dare with a mystical twist!

"Fun and rollicking..."
-Young Adult Books Central

Nova and the Charmed Three
Can Nova rock her way past Ivy and into Joe's heart?

Yumi Talks the Talk
Nova's best friend Yumi gets a big surprise!

Carmen's Crystal Ball
Carmen Bernstein, pet psychic, is open for business.

Bella Goes Hollywood
Bella's on the case of a Hollywood prankster.

Maya Made Over
Maya decides it's time to remake her image.

Rani and the Wedding Ghost
Can Rani exorcise the wedding ghost?
AUG 2007

Nova, Lost in Paradise
Nova and her band are off to Hawaii!
DEC 2007

HALLOWMERE™

Tiffany Trent

Come discover a dreamy, sinister, complicated world of fey.

Seven rathstones prevent the vampiric Unhallowed Fey from breaching
the seal between the Fey raths and the mortal world. The Unhallowed
will do anything to get the stones, which will give them power to destroy
the Elder Fey and regain dominion over humanity—and the only
ones standing in the way of the overwhelming power of the
Unhallowed are a group of teenaged girls.

In the Serpent's Coils

Volume One

By Venom's Sweet Sting

Volume Two

DEC 2007

Between Golden Jaws

Volume Three

MAR 2008

And more to come in 2008!

Join the Knights as they battle monsters, solve mysteries
and save their town from certain destruction.

COLLECT THEM ALL!

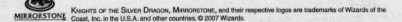